# WITCH WITH AN ATTITUDE

# WITCH WITH AN ATTITUDE

WITCH WARRIOR™ BOOK 12

TR CAMERON MARTHA CARR MICHAEL ANDERLE

LMBPN
DISRUPTIVE IMAGINATION®

## DON'T MISS OUR NEW RELEASES

Join the LMBPN email list to be notified of new releases and special promotions (which happen often) by following this link:

http://lmbpn.com/email/

This book is a work of fiction. All of the characters, organizations, and events portrayed in this novel are either products of the author's imagination or are used fictitiously. Sometimes both.



LMBPN Publishing
PMB 196, 2540 South Maryland Pkwy
Las Vegas, NV 89109

Version 1.00, April 2023
ebook ISBN: 979-8-88541-743-3
Print ISBN: 979-8-88878-323-8

THE WITCH WITH AN ATTITUDE TEAM

**Thanks to our JIT Readers:**

Christopher Gilliard
Dorothy Lloyd
Wendy L Bonell
Jackey Hankard-Brodie
Jeff Goode
Dave Hicks

**Editor**
SkyFyre Editing Team

# DEDICATION

For those who seek wonder around every corner and in each turning page. Thank you choosing to share the adventure with me. And, as always, for Dylan and Laurel, my reasons for existing.

*— TR Cameron*

# CHAPTER ONE

Cait Keane, US marshal, witch, and sometimes masked thief, complained, "Where are we, anyway?" She already had a partial answer to that question. Cait, her father, her two sisters, and her dragon companion Aza were on the magical planet Oriceran, in a region she didn't think she'd ever been to before.

The dragon flew above the tall grass, spilling a steady stream of mocking comments into her mind while the rest of them were forced to wade through it. Some of it reached shoulder height, and all of it was trying to snag on her tight-fitting leather armor and other gear. Her father was in the lead, which meant she had the distinct pleasure of both pushing through some of the annoying overgrowth on her own and getting smacked in the face by parts that whipped backward after his passage.

His deep laughter sounded from ahead. "We're several days' travel from the farthest dungeon we've ever explored together. I've never been this far in this direction by myself, either."

Aisling, behind her, chirped, "Sounds like a perfect afternoon outing to me. Maybe you should quit being such a whiner, Cait."

Cait sighed. This treasure hunt had been her idea, forced upon her by the dearth in her bank account that had resulted from the purchases necessary to pursue several unique and off-the-books projects during her time in Boston. The magical underground Purple Market in the city was fantastic for selection, but not for price. Since she couldn't be sure what circumstances might arise that would require quick access to funds, she'd requested this adventure.

Her father could probably have gained sufficient wealth to retire by now, based on his instinct for archaeological discoveries that included treasures both common and unique, but as he'd said on any number of occasions, he was in it for the knowledge, not the baubles. *Maybe if he'd focused on the money a little more, I could be relaxing at home today.*

Aza observed, *You are being whiny. Have you been possessed by a toddler?*

She replied, *Shut it.* His laughter mocked her again. Out loud, she asked, "And what kind of place are you leading us to this time, Mister Mysterious Won't-Tell-His-Daughters-Anything?"

He retorted, "Look for yourself."

Cait stepped out of the grass and stumbled at the transition onto a stone patio. Ahead stood an intact structure where she'd expected to find a ruin. It was a story and a half high, composed of massive stone blocks that she estimated were each five feet high and wide. Unlike other ancient structures she and her father had visited in the past, this one was made of precisely cut rock that created a flat surface rather than the more common roughhewn stone.

Moreover, the building did not appear to have suffered from its supposed abandonment. It looked clean enough to still be in daily use. She took in the double doors that ran from the ground to the top of the first story. They appeared to be made of solid gold, although realistically, it was more likely some Oriceran equivalent. Above the metal slabs was a wide rectangular block with a facade that had multicolored gears turning slowly on it. Brianna, the last to step out from the grass, asked, "What makes them move?" Her leather armor was crisscrossed with battle scars from training, and her long, curly red hair was pulled back in a knot.

Her father, who had advanced to the door and was peering upward, replied, "Magic. They're not attached to the building." He stroked his short gray beard as the rest of them joined him and discovered that the gears were indeed free-floating.

Cait asked, "I don't suppose you know another way in?"

"Nope. This is the first time I've been close to the place."

Aisling said, "Maybe it's as easy as pulling them open?" She walked up to the doors, and her voice darkened. "Oh. No handles. Or anything, actually. Flat slabs of metal. Great. I'm officially calling your preparations into question, Father." Her younger sister's armor was almost as pristine as hers, and at the moment, Cait envied her shorter hair. Like hers and Brianna's, it was red, but straighter than her older sister's and wavier than hers.

Cait suggested, "Brianna, why don't you bang your head against them until they open?"

Her sister turned to shield the obscene gesture she threw at Cait from their father's view.

Cait laughed, and Aza said, *Three circles that look like gears are arranged in front of the doors. You're too close to see them, I think. They're made of a slightly different-colored stone.* She looked down and saw nothing notable, but after walking to the side under the dragon's guidance, she spotted the boundary where one color ended and the next began. She pointed the arrangement out to the others, and they each stood on one.

After several seconds, the blocks at her feet glowed. Lines stretched out to connect her gear, which was on the left, with Aisling's in the center. A beam shot across the patio from that position to the doors, but nothing further happened. Brianna called from the opposite side of the arrangement, "What the hell?"

Aza laughed in her mind. *You are gears. Turn.* With a great deal of shouted coordination, several insults, and a number of wry comments, they all managed to turn in the appropriate directions at the same time. A pulse of magic from each outer gear hit the center one and progressed to outline the doors. They swung open without a sound.

Her father said, "Well done. I knew you three could work together if you put your minds to it."

Aisling stepped up next to him to peer inside and quipped, "You really should have given me smarter sisters."

Cait's path converged with Brianna's, and she muttered, "You hit her with the shillelagh, and I'll kick her legs out so she falls on her face."

Her older sister grinned. "Good plan. Her smugness deserves a good smack or three."

They did nothing of the sort, only followed Aisling and her father inside. Aza landed beside Cait as she walked into a huge chamber that called to mind a throne room but lacked the pivotal object. A strip of colored stone wide enough for them all to walk abreast led forward and bisected the room.

It was not a tall space, but skylights cut into the roof permitted sufficient light to penetrate that it felt bigger than it was. Cait stepped off the path and wandered to the left to investigate one of six narrow structures she'd at first thought were columns, three of which were on each side of the room. Closer examination revealed them to be pedestals with giant statues on top. As she neared one, she corrected that assumption as well. *Statue isn't the right word for these things.*

The objects were arguably human-shaped, but instead of representing flesh and bone, they were constructed from metal rods, slabs, and gears. The figure was uniformly technological in appearance until her eyes reached the head, where a human face was visible. Male, with dark hair framing his face but not spreading beyond the apparent projection and eyes closed as if asleep. The visage appeared to be middle-aged, judging by the modest number of lines on its skin. She breathed, "What the hell is that?"

Aza replied, *Not sure, but the other five are similar to it.* She paced through the room to examine each as her family members did the same. Once they had all taken a good look at the figures, they gathered in the center of the room, standing on the colored strip as if it was a bastion of predictability in a strange world.

Brianna asked, "Do you think those were the folks who worked here? Or some of them?"

Her father shrugged. "I'm guessing so. Why else bother to give them faces? It seems like a monument to themselves."

Cait asked, "You don't think the people somehow transferred themselves into them, do you?"

Aisling, the technomancy expert of the group, replied, "Nothing I've ever read suggests that could happen."

Her father countered, "Some secrets have been lost over time. It's possible. Sentient weapons had to get sentient somehow, right?"

Cait frowned, and her hand dropped to the hilt of Eclipse, which was sheathed at her belt. She conveyed the question to it, and the dagger replied that she had no memory of the time before she was a dagger. Cait shared that with the others. Everyone nodded, but her father cautioned, "We need to keep an open mind about it. You never know."

They moved forward and found that the colored stone path ended at a wide platform with a pedestal in the middle supporting a large button. Aisling laughed. "That's not ominous. Brianna, you go first."

Her father cut off the inevitable argument by saying more loudly than necessary, "We'll all go together." They gathered around the center, Lewis pressed the button, and the lift smoothly descended into a shaft of the same flat stone that made up everything else.

The guardians of the room below came into view as

soon as the platform entered the space. The sighting gave them enough time to ready their weapons before the creatures ran forward and leapt onto the descending surface. Cait met the first creature to arrive with a baseball-bat-style whack of her shillelagh. The metal and wood amalgam transferred a magical blast of lightning to her opponent at the moment of connection, and electricity wreathed it.

Her foe stiffened, all four legs locking beneath its doglike body, its metallic jaw with its wickedly sharp teeth spread open. The robot dog, for that was what it was meant to be, fell onto its side. Cait reached for more power and hammered it with force magic, slamming blasts into it to knock the pieces apart. Beside her, Brianna had met her opponent with an almost identical smash and was now raining blows on it with her weapon. Her shillelagh was also enhanced, but rather than casting through it, her sister used her magic to increase its solidity so it would hit harder.

Both wore bracelets that incorporated the wood of their wands, and long training allowed them to direct the power through their hands. Her younger sister had chosen a different path and converted her wand into wooden rings that graced her right hand. Aisling wasn't using magic at the moment but had drawn both of the curved swords from her back and was slicing and stabbing at her foe as it tried to bite her.

Aisling's battle mode was pure precision and traded a focus on strength for balance and accuracy. Pieces flew from her opponent's body as she struck it. Cait often thought her family was an interesting mix. Brianna almost always opted for brute force, Aisling was her opposite, and Cait occupied the middle and selected the approach she considered best for a given situation. At this particular moment, she believed she was the strongest of the siblings by virtue of having two wands instead of one, plus a great deal of practical experience with different kinds of battle provided by her time in the marshals and her actions in Boston.

She turned to assist her father, who was using his shillelagh in a defensive fashion at Aza's side. As the robots attacked, her father blocked their efforts and provided Aza an opportunity to breathe fire or slash with his claws. He had increased to his maximum size, which meant he was bigger than Lewis if he stood on his hind legs. They made quick work of the remaining three before she could reach them to help. When all the dogs were down, Brianna observed, "That was hardly a challenge."

Aisling sighed. "After all we've been through, don't you know better than to tempt fate like that?"

Cait agreed wholeheartedly and gave a dramatic sigh. "Well, let's go find whatever horrible destiny Brianna's just summoned for us."

# CHAPTER TWO

Cait stepped off the platform, careful not to trip and fall on any fragments of robot dog, and looked around the room. The chamber seemed to be nothing more than a landing space for the elevator, with a single door on the left. She took point, and Aza appeared at her side the moment she began to move. The dragon's sharp senses, plus her mundane and magical abilities, had repeatedly proven to be effective at detecting traps before they activated them.

As they passed through the door, Cait stretched part of her magic forward to examine the room while another portion branched out along her connection to Aza and beyond to seek the presence of other creatures. A last bit of magic held her shillelagh in the air and tapped it on the floor ahead of them with a consistent beat.

She and Aza had never discerned exactly how their merged power operated—whether she borrowed a piece of the dragon's abilities or if their magics combined to create something new and different, or yet another mix. Ultimately, Cait didn't feel the need to over-analyze it. The process had kept them safe on countless occasions, and she'd come to trust it. More, using it was now as natural to her as breathing, and she couldn't imagine functioning without it.

A small part of her worried that someday Aza would want to go back to his life among the dragons and no longer be her constant companion. If that moment came, she wouldn't begrudge him anything that increased his happiness, but she hoped it would be a long time from now, if ever.

The large chamber they entered knocked her out of her internal reverie. After a few cautious steps, she stopped, focused on tapping the shillelagh on all the floor panels, and peered into each large shadow. When no danger presented itself, she called, "I don't sense any traps, but be careful. This looks like it could be a hazardous space."

Aisling walked in, laughed, and clapped her hands. "It's a workshop. A technomancy workshop by the looks of it, and a damned impressive one."

Cait scowled at her sister. "Which is exactly why it's dangerous. You're not the most sensible person in the worlds, and I imagine whoever worked here was just as goofy as you."

Aisling waved a hand as she turned to the nearest workspace. "You worry like an elderly gnome. Go away."

Aza observed, *She's a lot less worried than you are.*

Cait replied, *About this place, you mean? She's excited, if anything.*

*No. About everything. You could take a lesson.*

She countered, *Someone has to be practical.*

His laughter echoed in her mind. *Oh, yeah. You're the very picture of practicality.*

*You can shut up now, scaleface.*

Cait wandered over to one of the workstations her family hadn't selected. The space was organized with meticulous care, with precision tools in custom holders around the periphery of the slab of stone and metal that occupied most of the workspace. She muttered, "Likely to provide neutral influence on the object they're working on. The stone is probably inert to handle magic, and the metal grounded to handle electricity, power, or whatever animated those dogs."

She moved to the next workstation, which was almost identical to the first, then made a circuit of the room, looking over people's shoulders. When she'd examined them all, she observed, "They put their toys away before they left."

Aisling replied, "This whole building feels very well maintained. It hits me as a workplace rather than a living place."

Brianna asked, "Why live here underground? They could just portal in since no anti-magic is present to prevent it."

"I don't know. Cultists like to hang out together?"

Cait suggested, "Perhaps it's only a part-time cult. Nine-to-five, or only weekends."

Her father laughed. "This isn't a cult. It doesn't have the trappings. I agree that it's a workspace, or maybe home to a group of hobbyists with shared interests in technomagical research and development."

Aisling asked, "Like making statues with living faces and robot dogs?"

Her father scratched his stubbled cheek. "You have a point. Let's call it an extremist hobby group."

Cait shook her head. "When I tell Mom how ridiculous you're all being, she's going to have words for you." The others reacted with insults, and she drifted to the room's exit. Aza joined her as she stepped through to discover a hall stretching ahead of them. If she had her directions right, which she was generally proficient at, the corridor led back toward the front of the temple. She was pretty sure they weren't under the other portion but beside it. Unfortunately, her connection with Aza didn't work for directions, only beings. She frowned. "I didn't sense those dogs before we saw them."

Aza replied, *You're just realizing that now?*

*I'm apparently a little slow today.*

His mental voice changed from amused to serious. *That looks like a scorch mark ahead.*

Cait jerked her attention back to the moment and saw what he was talking about. Six feet in front of her, the right-hand wall was discolored. The difference was subtle enough that she might have missed it without her partner's warning. She ran her gaze across the area inch by inch, then decided precision would serve her less well than blunt power here. *More Brianna than Aisling for this one.*

She created force barriers along the walls, floor, and ceiling that stretched a few feet in both directions, centered on the mark. As she walked through the area, fire splashed into the shield to her left. Whether it was magical or mundane was unclear, but either way, her protection was sufficient. She turned back to the others, who had wandered into the hall, and ordered, "Protect yourselves as you move through."

Cait dropped her magic once she'd advanced far enough that the jet stopped. Aza asked, *Why not just shield the entire hallway?*

She replied, *That could set us up for a great defensive trick, a mundane trap that's activated by the use of magic. I've seen those before. Nine times out of ten, caution is the way to go.*

*What if this is the tenth time?*

*Quiet. It's my job to be the pessimist on this team.* The next trap was a pit that her careful telekinetic prods with the shillelagh revealed before they reached it. A force floor took care of that one. A few steps later, a flurry of spikes shot out of the far wall of the corridor. The barrage would have minced her if she hadn't snapped up a shield to block them. Aza probably would've been fine since his magical scales had so far proven capable of handling most of the attacks they'd faced, but she would have been a leaky pincushion.

At the end of the passage, the hall made a left turn. Cait followed it but stopped before she crossed the threshold into a large room to search for traps near the entrance. None presented themselves, so she led the rest of the group inside.

Aisling said, "I'm almost certain we're beneath the entry chamber. This one looks like it's about two-thirds that length but shifted so the frontmost third is under the stone patio outside. It's also taller, maybe ten feet."

That front area was well-lit in contrast to the overall dimness of the room. A figure filled the space from floor to ceiling in the center of that section. They made a slow approach with weapons drawn and stopped in a semi-circle to stare at it. The effigy appeared to be constructed of metal, but the way the appendages pulsed and shifted made it look like flesh.

It was a strange amalgam of shapes. Cait would've called it an octopus because of the tentacled limbs jutting from the center, except that from the chest up, it appeared humanoid. It had another of those living faces on it, but this one slipped between expressions, moving from pain to aloof condescension, then morphing into greater pain. Her father's voice was concerned as he said, "Okay. I take it back. It's definitely a cult."

Brianna was unperturbed. "One with the gems we need. If you can get past how disgusting it is, that thing is covered with stones. Mainly small ones, but they will still sell. I think the head might have some gems on top, too."

Cait remarked, "Well, let's do what we're here to do, no matter how gross it's going to be."

Aisling's words came out slower than normal when she spoke. "I'm not sure that's a good idea."

Brianna snorted. "That's what you always say."

"I'm usually right."

Brianna took a step toward the effigy, and the room plunged into darkness. Cait twisted to her right as three shafts of light stabbed down from above. Aza warned, *Same thing on the other side.*

The light flickered as the metal statues from the first room floated gently down inside the columns of illumination. They came to life as their feet touched the floor. Mechanical arms snapped up, and articulated fingers moved together and compressed into needle-pointed blades at the end of each arm. Additional sharp edges clicked outward along every part of the robot.

The faces were no longer sleeping, and the same words emerged from each of the six mouths in unison and echoed through the chamber. "Trespassers. Offer a last prayer to the gods you follow, for now you die."

# CHAPTER THREE

Aza charged forward and leapt into the air, flapping his wings hard to gain altitude. Unlike the chamber above, this one was at least two stories high, which gave him room to work. Below, Cait and her family were already on the attack, separating by instinct or practice to engage different targets. The seamlessness of their teamwork was always impressive to the dragon, even though it could never be as coordinated as his connection to Cait made theirs.

She and he had become so interdependent that he knew what she would do before she did it. Despite the danger threatening them, he chuckled internally. *And she knows what I'm going to do, which is usually annoying.*

In this case, he was charging the pair the others hadn't chosen. His role when they were outnumbered was to take on whoever was left over. Since only two robots were uncommitted, he would try to distract one while attacking another, which would be more satisfying than trying to divert a bunch of them by flying around. Unlike the fragile humans, wizards, and witches with whom he frequently partnered, Aza had mighty protection thanks to his scales and wasn't afraid to go up against anything.

That thought had just crossed his mind when the sword hand of the nearest robot slammed into his flank and sent him off course. The blade didn't penetrate, but the blow was powerful enough to knock him aside. As his second target's blade pistoned out and stabbed into one of his scales, it became apparent that their enemies were also accustomed to working together. *I guess that's fair, if irritating.*

The second weapon failed to pierce his scales too. He whipped around in a tight curve and rolled himself into a ball an instant before he slammed into the back of one of the mechanical monsters' heads. His target stumbled forward as the blow stole its balance. Aza uncoiled, flapped to stay in the air, and breathed fire at the other as it stabbed both pointed hands at him.

The human visage on his enemy's flat skull looked alarmed as his flames washed over it. But as the blades did nothing to him, his breath did nothing to his opponent. He flew upward before another swipe could catch him, then corkscrewed to face his enemies again. He angled toward an empty corner of the room, and they fulfilled his desire by following. *Okay, if hitting them in the head doesn't work, let's try something lower.*

When he reached the wall, he twisted, turned, and pushed off to angle down at his closest foe's legs. That enemy danced aside with an impressive display of agility but blocked the view of the other one, which gave Aza an opportunity. He snapped his teeth on the thing's leg and held on. It fell sideways as he flapped into the air, and for a moment, Aza thought it would be carried up with him. The weight would have made that impossible if not for the magic that gave him the power of flight in contravention of the laws of physics.

The strain caused the leg to snap, and the robot fell. Aza crowed to Cait, *That's one that won't be moving very fast anymore.* He spat out the limb and turned to engage the other. The rapidly swinging arms that resembled double circular saws gave an indication that his remaining upright enemy now saw him as a greater threat than it had a moment before.

---

Aisling's swords clashed against the mechanical's arms as it tried to separate her head from her body with dual diagonal strikes. Its physical strength was far greater than any human she'd ever faced, but training usually won out over raw power. She chose not to meet her opponent strength to strength but dodged, deflected, and used its strength and momentum against it to send the blades harmlessly downward.

Then she leapt into the air and slashed at its neck. The sword connected with a clang but didn't penetrate its armor. Her feet touched the floor, and she threw herself into a backward roll to avoid the blade that stabbed down and penetrated a foot into the block she'd just been standing on. *Holy hell, it's fast. Since the obvious targets are well-reinforced, time to try something else.*

Aisling let her right-hand blade fall to the floor and cast

a line of force magic, her imagination and will turning it into a flexible rope. With a snap of her fist and by focusing her intent on her power, she wrapped it around her opponent's legs. When it had made four loops, she yanked on the line with a twist of her body and a sharp pull with her magic. The robot fell and landed on its back with a floor-shaking impact.

She shouted, "Legs seem vulnerable," and ran at her fallen foe, whose lower limbs were still bound. She jumped across its body to avoid a strike from its bladed arms and stabbed her sword into its knee joint with both hands. Sparks flew as the spinning gear at that location was intercepted by the steel, and a moment later, the joint blew apart. A piece of shrapnel whipped up to cut a long line across her cheek. She flinched sideways without conscious thought, which put her in the path of another.

A frantic effort got her blade up in time to deflect the sword coming at her chest but didn't stop it. It sliced the side of her thigh, and she shouted in pain. A moment later, Aza flew over her and slammed into the thing's knee with his body rolled up into a ball. The joint was destroyed, and the robot fell. She called, "Thanks, buddy." *Damn. I could* really *use a dragon.*

Aisling stood, grabbed a healing potion, and took a swig to deal with the wound. The one she'd dropped moved, and her attention snapped back to it. The thing was attempting to lever itself up on one arm, which gave her a perfect opportunity. She punched with her fist, and a blast of force shot out of it and blew its elbow joint apart. The robot crashed down on its upper arm, which also shattered.

Aisling wordlessly shouted her success, then offered, "Go for the joints."

---

Cait had rushed at the one nearest her, hoping to dispatch it fast so she could help with the others. However, that plan hadn't worked out as she'd hoped. She'd attempted to smash it in passing as she ran by to attack from the rear, but her shillelagh only connected with its bladed hand, and her weapon went flying. The attempt to get behind it also failed when it displayed unexpected nimbleness for something so large and spun to track her.

She threw herself into a shoulder roll to avoid a horizontal slash from its weapon, then came to her feet and ran as it pursued. She dug Eclipse out of its sheath, spun with it raised, and blasted lightning through the dagger to cover the metallic frame of her enemy. It stopped as the electricity played over it, but when she dropped the spell after several seconds, it resumed its advance, seemingly unharmed. She shouted, "Electricity doesn't work."

Aza had already given her advice from his battle, and she saw Aisling yank one from its feet nearby. *So, low is the way to go. I can get behind that.* She summoned her shillelagh with telekinesis, then used a blast of force to hurl it at her enemy's knee. A subtle touch of magic kept it on target, and it struck true. The weapon blasted through the joint and caused the robot to fall.

Unfortunately, its momentum carried it forward, and she barely managed to conjure a wall of force in front of her to catch the blades it slashed at her as it went down. It scrambled at her in pursuit, and she kept the barrier positioned between them as she backpedaled. A frustrated growl escaped her since the thing that kept her safe also prevented her from attacking it. She looked for Aza, spotted him nearby, and sent, *Switch.*

The dragon replied, *On it,* disengaged from his opponent, and hurtled across the room to go after hers. In turn, she summoned the shillelagh to her hand and threw it again, using force magic to drive it into the knee of an upright robot. That foe, too, went down. She threw herself to the side with a reflexive scream of alarm as it launched a flurry of spikes at her.

Only belatedly did her brain put together that it had transformed its blades into fingers and shot them at her. Her hasty shield intercepted two, and she avoided six. The remaining pair punched into her chest but were stopped by her armor. She muttered a word of thanks to the tailor who had improved her Oriceran gear as she leapt to her feet, then launched herself in a shallow arc across the room on a burst of magic and came down feet-first on an enemy's head. She jumped up, blasted it with force magic again, and stomped as she landed. The metal caved in under her boots. She shouted, "Okay, who's next?"

There was no answer. Her allies had taken out the rest, although Brianna was apparently trying to pulverize hers, not content with having beheaded it. Shaking her head, she crossed to stand beside her father and gestured at her older sister. "I think you guys did something wrong with her."

Lewis laughed. "Nah. She's the one we raised right."

Cait gently punched him in the arm. "Enough bad jokes. Let's grab the gems and get out of here. What do you say?"

He grinned, hefted his shillelagh, and pointed its head at the effigy. "Good plan, but if that thing comes to life, I'm portaling away and abandoning you all."

She snorted in mock derision. "Wow. Such dedicated parenting."

"I'm old and wise. I know when to let my children handle things."

"Or you're a scaredy-cat."

He laughed. "Guilty as charged."

## CHAPTER FOUR

They'd returned to Ireland laden with two bulging backpacks of gems that would be sufficient to support her normal and extracurricular equipment needs. Cait had then collapsed into bed and slept the night through. Some of the stress she'd been carrying had eased during the adventure, which kept any bad dreams at bay. When her sticky eyelids finally separated, she felt more refreshed than she had in weeks. She sat up on the edge of the bed, yawned, stretched, and twisted to pat Aza, who was lying on his back, staring at her. She frowned, "What?"

He gave a heartfelt sigh. *Do you have any idea how loud you snore?*

Cait pinched the bridge of her nose with her thumb and index finger. "Seriously? I've been awake for less than a minute, and you're starting already?"

The dragon chuffed a laugh. *Can't argue with reality.*

She extended a fist and gave him a gentle bonk on the head. "Perhaps it would help if I knocked you unconscious for a while. You won't be able to hear me snoring then."

*Or you could just leave. Shower, maybe.*

"I showered last night. Quit making up stuff to complain about." He wriggled around, put his paws on her back, and pushed her off the bed. She landed on her backside on the floor and yelped in surprise. "*Ow.* Jerk."

He gave his dragon laugh again. *If you're not going to do us all a favor and shower, shouldn't you make breakfast?*

Cait took a fast shower and changed into comfortable clothes, running shorts and a ragged T-shirt, then headed downstairs. Her mother was working on breakfast, and Cait slipped into the kitchen beside her. Moira said, "Sounds like you had an adventure yesterday."

Cait busied herself with cutting a loaf of freshly baked bread into half-slices and piling them in a basket. "It was something. It's interesting to think people were doing magic and technology long enough ago that the place could've fallen into disuse."

"Did your father get a sense of who used it?"

"No. He said he couldn't place it, and you know how he hates to rush to judgment on anything. Aisling thought automated systems powered by magic but involving technology might be keeping the building clean and fresh. If so, it's pretty much impossible to tell when it was last used."

Her mother did one of the bits of magic Cait always enjoyed watching, levitating eight pancakes off a large griddle and flipping them with a flick of her wand. "Well, as long as you had fun and no one was permanently damaged, it's all good. Lewis says an investigation team from the university will be heading over to take a look at it." She shook her head with a laugh. "He's really something."

Cait covered the bread with a cloth to keep it warm, then grabbed the basket and several plates filled with other baked goods and carried them out to the dining area. Her father was sitting at one end of the table, reading an old-looking book. She asked, "Which university is going to investigate?"

His face registered confusion as he looked up from his pages, then he said, "Oh, right. I think Oxford for this one, actually."

"Highest bidders?"

Lewis laughed. "No, but it was in their archives that I found the information that led me to the location. So it only seems fair for them to get the first shot."

She set the last plate down. "They are going to pay something, right?"

"Of course. Archaeology doesn't fund itself." He said it with a playful aloofness that made her smile.

Cait returned to the kitchen and asked, "He's hanging around at home more than usual, am I right?"

Moira nodded. "With things as unsettled as they are, it's good to have him here."

"Did you ask him to?"

"I didn't have to. He knows what his family needs from him."

Light conversation continued throughout breakfast, pleasant and comfortable. Her sisters told the tales of their battles, and she shared hers. Aza made an appearance so everyone could sneak him something from their plates, which had become a ritual. They all knew the others were doing it, which made the sly maneuvers even more amusing. By the end of the meal, they were all stuffed. Cait said,

"I'm sorry to dampen the happy mood, but what do we know about the wolves?"

Her mother crossed her arms with a frown. "They haven't shown their faces for some time. It seems clear that they're waiting for something, but no one in the coven has a solid understanding of what that might be."

Lewis suggested, "For us to let our guard down?"

Brianna stated, "That's not going to happen. Eventually, they'll just attack anyway. We should go take them out before they find a moment to use to their advantage."

Aisling countered, "That is a great plan, except we don't know where they all are."

Brianna replied with a whistling noise. "Go locate them, little bird."

Aisling rolled her eyes. "I'm planning to spend the day scouting with Grayson. But locating one pack doesn't mean we've found all of them. While we head out to attack one, others could use that opportunity to hit the coven."

Cait listened to her family discuss strategies and tactics until a knock on the door interrupted the noise. She rose to answer it, expecting Sashura or Delsanra to be on the other side with some demand on her time, but it was Will. His bright eyes, as always, were the first thing she noticed about him. He was dressed in clean but well-worn hiking clothes. He smiled and asked, "Want to take a walk?"

She looked over her shoulder. Everyone was still engaged in the escalating arguments. "I'm clearly not needed here, so sure." She stepped outside and held the door open for Aza. He flew loops around the village as she and Will walked into the large grassy area in the center of the coven and meandered along its perimeter. She asked, "Are you here every weekend?"

He smiled, which made his handsome features even more attractive. He was only a bit taller than her, but it felt a little odd having to look up at him. "Only the ones when I know you'll be here."

The comment triggered a warm feeling in her chest. "So, it seems like despite having gotten to know me, you're still serious about this relationship thing, huh?"

A laugh preceded his words. "Yeah. I think I am."

"Good. I think I might be, too."

His head snapped around to stare at her, and his steps faltered. "Really?"

She stopped and met his eyes. "Really. But I'm not going to give up my work in Boston just yet."

"Portals make long-distance relationships fairly easy, you know?"

Cait pushed down her emotions in favor of seriousness. "I might have some secrets you won't like."

A corner of his mouth quirked into a smile. "Could be that I have the same."

"Do you?"

The grin materialized fully. "Maybe you'll find out."

Cait laughed. "Fair enough." They walked and talked for almost an hour before she bade him farewell and headed back into the house. She went up to Aisling's room because her sister had mentioned that she'd like a quiet word. She knocked on the door, received a muffled "Come in" from inside, and opened it. Aisling sat cross-legged on the bed, her eyes half-lidded.

Cait said, "I can come back in a bit."

Aisling shook her head. "No, hang on. I'm landing. Grayson needs to recharge for a few minutes anyway." Her eyes opened fully, and she rose to her feet and stretched. "The bird isn't the perfect tool for this sort of thing. I think you should let me partner with Aza from now on. He's sure to like working with me more."

Cait stuck out her tongue. "No. He's mine. Build yourself a dragon friend."

Her sister laughed. "Maybe I will. If I do, he'll be way better than yours."

"I'm telling Aza you said that."

"He won't believe you. He knows how much you lie and how much I love him."

Cait grinned, thinking about the dragon. He would take her sister's side just to be a jerk. "Don't force me to kill you. What did you want?"

"Right." Aisling moved to her desk and opened a metal case that sat on the top. Inside it were four small metal vials the size of Cait's thumb. "I drew some blood when your friend was poisoned and used it to make a counter agent. Then, I built on that with magic. These should be antidotes for most poisons that have anything in common with the sample. I can't guarantee it, but if you're in trouble, I think they'll work. At worst, they won't do any additional harm."

Cait accepted the metal case. "Will they work on humans, too?"

Aisling nodded. "The magical enhancements won't do anything for them, but the base formula should."

Cait gave her sister a hug. "You're amazing. Thank you."

"I know, but it's always nice to hear. Now go away and let me get back to my all-important reconnaissance."

That night found Cait on Croagh Patrick. When she finished her meditation and opened her eyes, the fox was waiting, as she'd hoped he would be. He paced within the confines of the ward circle in fits and starts. He seemed less present to her, more spectral, as if some of his essence had been lost. She remarked on it, and he stopped moving and laid down on the ground. He looked tired, which was a quality she'd never seen him display.

He replied, "I feel thin. Something is wrong to the east. Not close by, but not that far away, either. It's causing me to weaken."

"Will you be able to continue to defend this place?"

His muzzle moved slowly from side to side as he shook his head. "Once, I would have been positive I could. Now, I am not as confident."

The words filled Cait with concern. "I'm going to ask my family to watch over the mountain."

The fox laid his chin on his paws and looked at her with sad eyes. "That would be for the best. I don't know how much longer I'll be able to manifest here, and once I'm gone, this place of power will be in great danger."

# CHAPTER FIVE

Cait made it back to Boston in time to shower and dress in her most comfortable suit and not be late for work. She passed through the doors to the outer office and vectored immediately for the coffeemaker at the side of the room. Laughter came from behind her as Sabrina asked, "Late night?"

Cait waved vaguely. "Life is exhausting. If I'm to avoid killing everybody in sight, I'm going to need caffeine."

"Noted. I'll just wait until you've woken up a bit to attempt actual conversation, shall I?"

"Smart plan." The exchange put a smile on Cait's face, and she wandered over to the infomancer's desk as soon as her cup was full. "Did you have a good weekend?"

Sabrina shrugged. "It was fine, though not success-filled."

Cait replied, "It's the weekend. You should be relaxing, not trying to succeed."

From his spot around her neck where he'd disguised himself as a necklace, using his always astonishing shape-shifting abilities, Aza commented, *Maybe you should take your own advice.*

She countered, *Maybe you should shut up.*

Sabrina said, "I mostly relaxed, but I decided to find out a bit about the Cui Siwang."

Cait pointed a finger at her friend. "I very specifically told you not to do that."

Sabrina laughed, got out of her chair, and perched on the edge of her desk. As always, she was clad in black, this time in a gorgeous vintage dress with truly obnoxious black-and-white striped stockings covering her legs. Combat boots finished her apparel, and today she'd added several pieces of bright silver jewelry, including clasps with skulls on them to hold her ponytails in place on the sides of her head. Cait said, "Well, I hope your infomancy skills are better than your listening abilities because those suck."

The infomancer grinned, clearly enjoying the banter. "Far better, but in this case, still not up to the task. I wasn't able to discover anything about their presence in Boston, which was the whole point of the run. I did get some background about their efforts in China as a consolation prize."

Cait sipped her coffee, wincing as she burned her tongue for the second time in the last two minutes. "What did you find?"

Sabrina leaned forward and lowered her voice. "The Cui Siwang is the real freaking deal. They've got their fingers in every pie you can imagine, legal and not. Picture the Mafia in America's past, only far more wide-reaching and violent."

"That's not a pretty thought. I can see why Yoshino's worried."

"Right? Getting into bed with those guys was a bad idea, and the only one that might be worse is going up against them. Oh, and speaking of scumbags, no new information on Victor Huff or Perpetuity, either. I did some digging specifically for political information, but aside from the fact that Huff is friends with and a donor to every politician in town, I wound up with a lot of nothing."

Garrett Bradley called in a baritone, "You ladies better stop gabbing and hop it to the conference room, or you'll be late for our meeting. You know how much the chief *loves* late arrivals."

Cait called back without looking, "On our way. Thanks, Dad." She crossed to her desk, dropped her purse in a drawer, and headed to the conference room. Clement was already seated on one side of the table. His blond hair always reminded her of a surfer's, which fit his low-key attitude well. Garrett was in the process of claiming the seat next to him. He looked tired, which she attributed to having spent the weekend with his family.

She took the chair across from him, leaving the one on her side closer to the door for Sabrina. Cait idly mused as she lowered herself into the chair with a groan that she'd never seen the other five seats at the table filled and that someone had been optimistic when they'd designed the conference room.

Sabrina entered, followed shortly by Chief Susan Clark. Her hair was pulled back in a loose ponytail, and her eyes were serious behind the lenses of her glasses. Her dark suit was a similar shade to Clement's but looked more expensive. Susan said, "All right. Anyone have anything burning that needs addressing?"

Clement quipped, "That's kind of a personal question, Boss, but I do have a twinge in my ankle. Maybe I should take the day off to get that looked at."

She shook her head and gave him a sad look. "Aren't you supposed to be the tough one of the group? Honestly, I didn't expect to find a bunch of babies up here in Boston. Do you need me to hire a nursemaid to watch over you, bubby?"

A wide grin spread across his face. "Would you, boss? I'd really like that."

Everyone laughed, and Susan snapped, "No," with false anger. All mirth left her voice as she said, "Then today will be all about coordinating with the city's other agencies to investigate the attack on the Thorns leaders."

Sabrina asked, "Leaders, plural? You think the bad guys went after them both?"

"Until such time as evidence proves it otherwise, it makes sense to assume that's the case."

Cait asked, "Has anyone seen Carl?"

Garrett answered, "Winston is in the wind, from what my contacts say."

"So, he could be dead."

Clement grunted at the notion. "I doubt it. That jerk's a survivor. All joking about Cait's questionable prisoner management abilities aside, it takes someone competent to get away from us the way he did. I don't know much about his partner, but I'm guessing we haven't seen the last of him. If they took him out, you'd think they'd want it to be known."

Susan nodded. "That's the prevailing opinion of almost everyone I've talked to about it as well. We have two questions at hand. First, who sent the Cui Siwang up against the Thorns, and second, where is Carl Winston, and what is he up to?"

Cait frowned. "Do we have confirmation that it was the Cui Siwang?"

"Close enough. Homeland Security thinks so, with a ninety percent probability attached. The other ten percent is a bunch of possibilities that looked ridiculous to me."

Sabrina said, "That's pretty decisive. Guess I know what I'll be doing today."

Susan nodded. "If you're thinking that's turning over every possible electronic stone in search of data about them, you're right. We've got less skilled infomancers handling the basics, so you can let your instincts guide you to something better than they'll be able to discover."

"Consider me on it."

Susan looked at Garrett and Clement. "You two, visit the crime scene again, talk to the people you know, and see if you can find anything that's not being shared with me." They nodded. Susan turned to Cait. "You have the most enjoyable task of all."

Cait winced at the headache that was making itself known inside her skull. "Meeting with Yoshino to find out what she knows."

"Got it in one." Susan stood and clapped her hands. "All right, get to it, people. Time matters on this one, and the clock is ticking."

After several calls, Cait managed to get hold of someone who could connect her with Yoshino. The fact that she'd had to work her way up the chain suggested that the Dragons were having a busy day, which made sense. With the city's other major gang reeling from the loss of their leader, Yoshino's people would doubtless be searching for weak spots to exploit. *And, if Carl Winston is still alive, probably searching for him, too, to change that status.*

When she finally received a return call from Kono Zhelan, it was past lunchtime. He agreed to a meeting and gave her a place to be and a time to be there. She followed the directions, and when the black SUV pulled up to the curb, she opened the rear passenger door and climbed inside. A shiver of alarm ran through her at the discovery that Kono was in the backseat, positioned in the middle to separate her from Yoshino, who sat behind the driver. Cait frowned. "Is there something I should know?"

Yoshino replied, "After the attack by the Cui Siwang, my guards became less trusting. Kono would have preferred we not meet in person, but I believed you deserved that measure of respect. So, a compromise."

"Should I assume that the reason the person in the passenger seat is twisted the way they are is that they're pointing a gun at me through the seat?"

The other woman smiled. "Probably wise to do so."

Cait nodded. "In Kono's position, I would likely have insisted on the same. The word is out that the Cui Siwang were behind the attack on the Thorns' leadership. I'm here to ask two things. First, what can you tell me about them that you haven't already shared?"

"Very little. I'm sure you've done your research and

know the basics. All my contacts have been with one of the sons of *the* Cui Siwang, as their leader is called. Shao is the name I know him by. I believe he comes to town with some regularity."

"That's something to go on. Thank you. Second, do you know if Carl was also targeted in the attack?"

Yoshino sighed. "Had the soldiers listened to me, he would have been. However, they were focused on recouping the honor of their comrades, who had failed in their previous attempt on the woman. I am not sure, but my impression is that the attack was likely on her alone."

"Which brings up a third thing. I don't suppose they've left town, have they?"

Yoshino's expression turned darkly serious. "Quite the contrary. From what my people say, any losses they incurred have been made good and additional forces have arrived. They have also moved out of the space I loaned them."

"Do you know what they're planning?"

The other woman winced as if she were in pain. She opened her eyes, met Cait's, and replied, "Nothing that will be good for my people, your people, or the citizens of Boston, I imagine."

# CHAPTER SIX

Sabrina had spent several hours reviewing her programs and tools, as she did most Mondays, to be sure they were at maximum potency. Part of her weekend routine was to visit the infomancer boards and search for new approaches to hacking, new tools, and evidence of vulnerabilities in common programs or infomancy tactics. It never failed to amuse her that she might be talking to someone she'd wind up facing inside a system on another day, sharing her secrets in exchange for theirs.

That was how the game was played, and the best part about it was that, though she fought many battles, they were bloodless. The risk of discovery and attack in the flesh was present but generally not a concern. An infomancer would be reluctant to give that kind of information to an employer, both due to the common experience they all shared and because it could put them at direct risk from the rest of the community. Some rules you didn't mess with, even if you mostly ignored the others, and taking a virtual conflict out into the real world was one of them.

Sabrina was doubly protected since any attempt to trace her back to her equipment would be cut off by a fail-safe in Washington, DC. That last resort switch would prevent someone doing a backtrace from knowing it was the Boston office that was after them. It was a backup plan she'd arranged long before but had never used since she was quick to disengage when she determined that a situation exceeded her current ability level.

By three o'clock that afternoon, she was ready. She stepped into her changing room and put several streaks of makeup across her face, two stretching from one cheek to the other over her nose and a third in a vertical line from her lower lip down her chin. It was her minimal version of battle dress, and it helped focus her mind and reinforce her will by reminding her that she was a warrior at the height of her ability and power.

She settled into the custom form-fitting chair in front of her computers and set her hands on the keyboard. A moment later, her view of the real world was replaced by the virtual landscape of the web, and she flew above it like a high-speed drone in terrain-follow mode, dipping and dodging to stay close to the ground and avoid detection. Landmarks flashed by beneath her, which she recognized as accesses to certain systems. That confirmed that she was moving in the correct direction.

Her assumption was that whatever servers the Cui Siwang used would be located within China's physical and virtual borders. Several things suggested that likelihood, including covertly entering the country's virtual space, was a not-insubstantial challenge. "The great firewall of China" was a standing joke among Western infomancers, but it was never said with derision.

The main pipelines were well-guarded and highly surveilled. The hidden breaches were dangerous at best and subject to discovery by the government's aggressive official infomancers. And though no irrefutable evidence existed, many of those she'd talked to about it shared the belief that infomancers caught trying to break in through the firewall had been killed in the real world. That might have stopped a more conservative infomancer from making the attempt, but Sabrina trusted her ability to bail out before trouble could reach her.

She'd been in and out of the country's virtual territory several times using the same routine. She attached herself to normal traffic, activated concealment, and rode it through the outermost access. Once inside the boundary, she broke away and navigated to a less congested stream, a banking connection between Chinese financial institutions and certain ones in Switzerland. An official channel existed for such things but didn't eliminate the need for this unofficial route for secretive transfers that carried her further into the Chinese servers.

Next, she dove into a heavily populated data stream and let it carry her presence along while she soaked up information about her surroundings. Once she determined her location, she shifted to a transit line headed in that direction and then another. Finally, she reached what she thought was a potential way into the Cui Siwang's virtual stronghold and pushed more magic into the system to take "physical" shape.

Her avatar materialized in a stereotypical countryside

scene. She was on a dirt path with meticulously tended crops on both sides. The colors were too vivid for real life —the sky a note too blue, the plants too lush in their vibrant green. A castle stood ahead of her at a distance that prevented her from judging its size. It resembled a pagoda, with the traditional smooth curves and sharp points, and was painted in reds and golds that shimmered in the abundant sunlight.

She looked down at herself and saw that she was dressed in peasant clothes, with pants that didn't go past her calves and a short-sleeved shirt that had seen better days. Her avatar's skin was darkened by the sun, and a rotation of her hands showed calloused palms. She muttered, "Well, that kind of puts me in my place, doesn't it? I think not."

Sabrina called up a history book for the region in her system and looked up more appropriate garb. An effort of will redrew her avatar in the guise of an aristocrat. She chose to be male, aware that at the moment of Chinese history when such a castle would exist, women would not be seen as people of power. Comfortable and ornate sandals protected her feet, and robes of gold and crimson, a muted echo of the castle ahead, covered her from neck to ankles.

She walked slowly to take in her surroundings. When she drew nearer to the castle, the absence of an outer wall surprised her. Renderings of such places that she'd seen almost always had some sort of barrier protecting the compound, which usually included the castle and several other support buildings. When she reached the location in which she would have placed that outer wall if she'd been in charge, movement in the corner of her eye caused her to freeze in place.

A yellow and orange Chinese dragon, long and sinuous with glorious curving whiskers on the front of its snout, slithered across the road from one green field to the next. When it had vanished into the crops, she whistled and held out her hand, and a small songbird appeared in it. She threw the program into the air and looked out through its eyes.

Rather than a wall of stone, the compound was protected by seven patrolling dragons. From her vantage point above, the ripples they made in the plant life gave a clear indication of their positions. Their speed would prohibit anyone from sneaking past them. *An appropriate first trial.*

Sabrina lifted her chin and advanced, her pace measured and her demeanor relaxed. She paused as a dragon emerged to block her path. It slithered up to her and rose, looking down upon her. She gazed up, her eyes traveling over its green-scaled belly and its sharp white teeth to its jade eyes. It stared at her, and she stared back, her mind focused on her breathing as its program and hers interacted.

After several moments, it dropped again and resumed its patrol. Her concealment programs had proven stronger than its detection abilities. It might have seen her as the aristocrat she purported to be, or she might have vanished from its view. What happened on the other end of the simulation was impossible to know.

Sabrina continued forward and noted long buildings to the left and right with covered porches and beautifully carved red-stained dark wood. It was a sight out of a history book. She climbed the stairs that led to the castle's entrance and stopped at the top. A pair of identical samurai stood on either side of the golden entrance door, holding long spears that crossed before it. They didn't acknowledge her presence, but the spears they held didn't part to permit her access to the door, either.

A silent struggle ensued as her programs fought them, but they stayed in place. The impasse left Sabrina with two obvious options. The first was to attack the samurai and breach the castle that way. She was confident she could defeat them, although they must be powerful AIs if they were holding off her infiltration programs since no AI she'd come up against was strong enough to stand against her for long, but that would risk discovery.

Her other option was to leave without alerting the system that she was more powerful than its defenses appeared to be. She chose a middle ground and sent a moderately stronger version of her infiltration software at them. Their arms trembled, but the spears did not uncross.

Sabrina's avatar bowed, then turned and walked away as if defeated. For the moment, her foes could enjoy their victory, but only for the moment. The knowledge she'd gained would allow her to better customize her programs for the next run and for the ones after that if needed until she found a way inside.

She logged out and leaned back with a smile. "I do so love a worthy opponent."

# CHAPTER SEVEN

The day after her visit with Yoshino, Cait teamed up with Garrett to make the rounds of his contacts. He hadn't been able to arrange a meeting with the gang task force the previous day because they were busy leading the Thorns investigation, so that was their first stop.

The unit was operating out of temporary quarters in an old city-owned warehouse to accommodate their increased numbers. The level of gang activity in Boston had necessitated more personpower to maintain the status quo as the Thorns' efforts to consolidate the smaller ones into their own organization continued.

Cubicles occupied a third of the giant building's floor, providing temporary homes for the team's personnel. Movable walls on wheels sectioned off a space to use as a planning room, and the receptionist led them to it. The walls were covered with pictures of known agents of the Dragons, the Thorns, and now, the Cui Siwang. The fourth wall had information about the leaders of the few smaller gangs that hadn't been snapped up by the Thorns during their rapid expansion.

A portly man in a sharp suit came in carrying a bundle of file folders and dropped them on the table with a thump. "These are copies of everything we have on the Cui Siwang. Electronic versions were sent to your office a couple of minutes ago, but I know Garrett there likes to do things the old-fashioned way due to his advanced age."

Garrett laughed. "A hearty hello to you too, Dirk." The two men met in a hug that involved a good deal of back pounding, then separated. Garrett explained, "We were partners way back when for a couple of years. Kept each other alive and maintained the peace. All that good stuff."

Cait asked, "So, are any of the stories he tells true?"

Dirk laughed. "I doubt it. I did all the hard stuff. He just hung out."

"That's definitely not how he tells it."

Dirk put his hands on his hips. "You mean to tell me he's still taking credit for all my hard work?"

Cait nodded with her most innocent expression. "Yep."

Garrett pointed at her. "Stop lying." He traversed the finger to his former partner. "And you! The only place you did all the work was in your head. Things were pretty even back then, as I recall."

Dirk groaned without feeling. "Not like now. Now *we* all do all the work, and no one under the top two or three gets any credit."

Garrett sat down and grabbed a folder. "Amen." He opened and perused it. Cait took one and sat down beside him to review the materials inside. After several minutes, he said, "Damn. These people aren't messing around."

Cait nodded. "Right? Violent as hell."

Dirk had taken a seat across the table. "Exactly. Having them in the city is not a good thing."

"Do you know anything more than what's in here?"

The man shrugged. "After reading everything we have, we're of the official opinion that all of them, or at least most, are magicals. That's not the case in China, but from what we've seen here, their street soldiers have magic."

Cait nodded slowly. "That makes sense. They would need it to take down someone like Cynthia."

"Exactly what we thought."

Garrett sighed. "So they're armed, magical, and exceedingly dangerous. Do I have it right?"

Dirk flipped the folder he was looking at closed. "That about sums it up."

Cait and Garrett headed out to eat at a small Indian restaurant nearby. She drank tea while he raided the basketful of naan and chomped down in a mix of pleasure and frustration, to judge by his expression. After he'd polished off two pieces, he paused to say, "You know, things used to make sense. Sure, Boston had its criminal element. Always. Every big city does."

He pulled out another piece and waved it as he spoke. "Even when it was the Roses and the Dragons, things operated according to their own twisted logic. Then that damn Carl Winston got involved, and everything went to hell." He chewed, swallowed, and flashed his mocking smile at her. "You really should have kept him on a leash."

Cait reached into the breadbasket, pulled out a piece of naan, and threw it at his head. He caught it, laughing. She said, "You're not wrong. A lot of trouble could have been averted if we had kept that guy under control. We didn't, so complaining about it at this point doesn't do any good."

"You'll need to talk to the PDA next."

She frowned. "Why?"

"They concern themselves with magical threats. The Cui Siwang is now believed to be one. It's time for you to visit your buddy Paul Andrews."

"He's most definitely not my buddy."

Garrett shrugged and leaned back as their food arrived. "Well, whatever he is to you, I've got other things to do this afternoon, so he's yours. Maybe give Clement a call. He might be interested."

Not only was Clement interested, he was downright happy when they made contact with Paul Andrews and discovered that he, his partner Natalie Hood, and the rest of his people were out on a training mission in the suburbs. They took Clement's sports car, and he wove in and out of slower traffic on the highway, disdaining the brakes in favor of veering from lane to lane. When they arrived, Cait stumbled out of the car and scowled over the roof at him. "You're a maniac. You know that?"

Clement laughed. "That was nothing. You should see me in heavy traffic."

"I'm driving on the way home."

He snorted. "No chance."

"Well, then I'm not riding back with you." Cait was joking but was also serious. She'd likely portal home to gain an extra hour in her day. She needed to restock on food at the fish market, among other less pressing errands.

They walked to a squat building and found Paul Andrews and Natalie Hood standing outside, with their team positioned to make an assault on the building. The two leaders wore business suits and stood away from the folks in tactical gear who were lined up beside the door. Cait and Clement stopped beside them, and Paul gave them a nod of acknowledgment. Then he shouted, "Weapons free."

The lead agent pressed the button on a device in his hand, and the door blew off the building. They all ran inside, and Cait was surprised not to hear gunfire from within. After several seconds, shouts of "Clear" came from the interior. Paul asked, "Results?" He was quiet for a moment, then added, "Good job. Let's get another door mounted and try it again."

When he turned to face them, Cait noticed the earpiece she'd guessed he was using. He shook her hand, then Clement's, and Natalie did the same in reverse. Cait asked, "No live rounds?"

He shook his head. "Entirely electronic. Lasers and receivers. Much safer that way. Well, except for the door, obviously."

"Seems like a good plan."

He grinned. "Want to try?"

Cait laughed. "Not right now. We've got other stuff to do. But sometime, I'd be glad to play the villain if you want."

Natalie replied, "That would be a great challenge for the team. We should totally do that."

"I can probably get my overly intelligent sister to figure out how to emulate lasers with magic to work with your system."

Paul clapped once. "That sounds awesome. Let's talk

about it later this week and set a date. I presume you're not here for a social call, though, correct?"

Clement asked, "What do you know about the Cui Siwang?"

"They're of interest to us because they're clearly a magical threat."

Cait said, "True, although maybe not all of them, according to our infomancer. Definitely the soldiers."

Paul scratched his chin. "I don't suppose we're lucky enough that they were just here for Cynthia, right?"

She shook her head. "Not if Yoshino is correct. She says we've got more of them on the ground already. I imagine they're going to go after Carl next, but who knows? Yoshino wouldn't give me a clear answer as to what she thought they were up to, but it seems to me like they see themselves as more than just hired help."

Natalie said, "Well, hell."

Paul chuckled. "That about sums it up." His eyes came back to Cait's. "You're awfully friendly with the Dragon Lady."

Cait replied, "Freely acknowledged." Most of the people in law enforcement called Yoshino the Dragon Lady. She figured the woman would appreciate it if she knew.

"Do you think that compromises you?"

Cait pushed her hair out of her face with both hands. "I sure as hell hope not."

Paul gave another of his sardonic laughs. "Fair answer."

"I'm not deluding myself that she's a friend or is always honest with me. I just don't have anything better right now."

Clement added, "That's the problem. The marshals don't have anything better, either."

Natalie replied, "Same here."

Paul said, "It is what it is, and more information is usually better than the alternative, but be careful. The rumor is that she's good with a sword."

Cait had no doubt that Yoshino was dangerous in a multitude of ways, swords included. "I hope to never find out."

# CHAPTER EIGHT

After stopping at the fish market as planned, Cait portaled back to her apartment and started cleaning. She hadn't done that in a while because of the many projects stealing her time. After an hour, Sabrina called, and Cait asked, "What's up, computer chick?"

The other woman laughed. "Oh, not all that much. Just discovered something interesting about the Cui Siwang, but you probably wouldn't be interested in that."

"I am most definitely interested. What do you know?"

"Turns out that one of the important people in the organization has made a bunch of trips to Boston. Private jet, but the same one each time, so once I tripped to it, it wasn't difficult to track."

She frowned at a sudden burst of noise across the channel. "Where are you?"

Sabrina laughed. "At a rooftop bar, looking at the building where the guy's penthouse is."

Cait's pulse quickened. "Really?"

"Really. While I wouldn't say I'm doing an amazing job

of surveillance, in part because the bartenders are pretty cute, it doesn't look like anyone's home. Just a couple lights on here and there."

Cait rose and moved toward her bedroom. "Easy access?"

"That's where things get tricky. I haven't been able to find out anything useful. The people who own the building have a rather secure system. Almost as if the people who live there don't want to be discovered."

"Imagine that." She put on a business suit rather than the infiltration gear she'd planned to don but switched to her Lexi hair, then slapped on some makeup. "Okay. Tell me where it is. I think I need to take a look."

Sabrina gave her the location, and Cait portaled to a spot nearby. As she walked the two blocks to her destination, she focused on getting into her alter ego's headspace, leaving Marshal Cait Keane behind in favor of the mysterious and adventurous Lexi Matthews. The building, like many in the city, was a combination of retail and residential. The first floor was given over to a restaurant, a bar, and a coffee shop, all of which were likely patronized by those who lived there but also accessible to the public.

She walked through a large revolving door into a beautiful two-story lobby with a glass chandelier positioned in the exact center over a round gold fabric couch that surrounded a statue of a heavily muscled male archer, his bow pointing at the far side of the room. She made a show of looking at the place, mainly staring at the chandelier and statue while carefully examining her surroundings out of the corner of her eye.

The far end was a wall of five elevators, the metal all

polished gold or brass. *Probably gold in this place.* Two tough-looking men in suits flanked the door of the center car. The other lifts were larger, and she presumed the guards were watching the one that led to the exclusive floors. When their attention turned to her, she pulled out her phone, took a picture of the chandelier, and walked into the lounge.

It was all dark wood and brass, with a wraparound bar to the left and seating areas ahead and to the right. She took the nearest empty seat and ordered a drink, gauging the available sight lines. Nowhere in the lounge provided an angle on the center elevator, so watching for the Cui Siwang representative as she'd planned wouldn't work. It would almost certainly be impossible to pick him out of the general traffic without something else to go on. She did have a good view of the entrance, but without knowing what he looked like, that wouldn't be of much help.

Cait called Sabrina. "Do we know what your mystery man looks like?" It wasn't a great code, but it would do.

Sabrina replied, "Working on that now, but at the moment, no."

"All right. Well, we need to get a drink at this bar sometime. It's amazing, but I guess I'll be getting home." She downed her drink, paid her bill with cash, and headed for the street. A few minutes later, she was back in her apartment.

Aza had stayed behind during her reconnaissance. *Find anything useful?*

"Yeah. Trying to figure out who he is at ground level is a no-go. There's no way to watch the elevator, which is the only clue we'd have to separate him from anyone else who lives there."

"So, what's the plan?"

Cait pulled her infiltration suit out of her safe. "Breaking and entering, of course."

She slipped into the suit and placed Aza in his cuff form around her bicep inside it. She pulled her cowl down, and the suit went through its self-diagnostic, then reported that its systems were all working properly. She had Eclipse and a taser with two reloads but didn't plan to take anything more powerful than that. Her plan was to take a look but not to act unless she got definitive evidence that their person of interest was out of the building.

Cait planned to use a portal to get to the roof of a nearby structure that provided a line of sight on the top of the target building. It was a strange angle, and her portal would be a few feet over the surface and uncomfortably close to the edge, but it was what she had. She focused and summoned her magic, but the portal failed to open. A frown accompanied her second attempt as she wondered if she'd messed something up, but again, no rift manifested.

She grumbled, "Well, hell. They must have anti-magic emitters up there. Clever bastards. Okay, Aza, go take a look." She unzipped the suit and pulled the cuff out. She tossed it in the air, and it transformed into the dragon, who grew in size as he flapped away. She lost sight of him almost immediately as his camouflaged scales did their work, but her connection to him meant she always knew where he was. He didn't land when he reached the roof but flew a circle around the surface. *Thank goodness anti-magic emitters don't affect his ability to fly.*

He sent, *Lots of equipment and stuff, but all the accesses are small. You wouldn't fit.*

She replied, *No doors or hatches or anything?*

*None.*

Cait ground her teeth in frustration. *Seems impractical. They'd have to bring maintenance people in by helicopter, but I guess when you have the money and an obsession with security, it's not a ridiculous choice.*

She sensed Aza flying a wider loop. He said, *I could smash through the windows.*

*No. We don't want to warn him he's being looked at. We need the information but want to avoid spooking him. It would be bad if he fled back to China before we can get it.* She thought about it for a second, then shook her head in frustration. *All right, buddy. Let's call it a night and take some time to think this through. We'll be back.*

# CHAPTER NINE

Cait spent every spare moment of the next day seeking a solution to the problem of getting the information they needed while Sabrina searched for pictorial evidence of who the Cui Siwang representative might be. When the end of the day came, each had found what they were looking for, sort of. They met at Sabrina's dining room table with a pizza but no wine.

The infomancer set a tablet on the table. It displayed three images, all of men who looked to be Chinese nationals in their thirties or maybe late twenties. Cait was notoriously bad at judging ages. The infomancer explained, "I managed to break into the security cameras at the airport. I think I was undetected, but even if they did see me, they'll think it was a generic hack attempt."

Cait interrupted, "Was that dangerous?"

Sabrina waved a hand. "No more so than most of the stuff I do. These are three images that show up most often in correlation with the landings and departures of the plane that we've identified."

"If one of them is our guy, who do you think the others are?"

Sabrina chewed a bite of pizza before replying. "Possibly assistants, maybe decoys, but probably guards. I would be shocked if the three of them aren't together most of the time. It was that way in the security footage, and they were smart enough not to be in the same arrangement each time, which prohibits us from guessing who the target is. I think Shao is the middle one."

Cait asked, "You weren't able to get pics?"

"No. He's not a very public figure, apparently."

She idly tapped the center picture. "What makes you think this is our guy?"

"Something about the way he carries himself. His confidence, maybe. I don't know. Call it a hunch." Sabrina played a video and pointed out the telltales she'd noticed.

"Okay. That's good enough for me. Best case, all three of them will be together."

Sabrina asked, "What's the plan?"

"I can't sneak inside, so I'll be the lookout. Once we see these guys leave, Aza goes in through the roof with the smallest access unit you've got, and you try to hack whatever he finds inside."

The infomancer grinned. "I love how important I am to your plan. This is gonna cost you so many pizzas."

Cait laughed. "Guess it's a good thing I went back to Oriceran last weekend. Anyway, do you have something that'll work for this?"

"I do."

"And are you free tonight?"

The other woman rolled her eyes. "You know my dedication to having a social life. Of course I'm free."

Cait stood. "Then let's get to it, shall we?" She took the hall back to her apartment, summoned Lexi's hair, and put on Lexi's makeup. She'd wanted to be unnoticed the last time she'd visited the place, but this time she intended to be obvious. It would make sense to those who bought into stereotypes that she might be on the prowl for a rich boyfriend, and she'd use that to her advantage.

A couple of women at the bar had fit that standard description, although she'd seen as many solo women there who looked like business people. The less competent she made herself seem, the less risk she'd face if she was noticed, or that was her guess. *The more they underestimate me, the better.*

She pulled out a bright blue dress she'd only worn once on a date with Shane and slithered into it. As she adjusted the straps, her mind wandered to her former sort-of-boyfriend, who was now on the West Coast. She'd been busy since his departure and knew he would be occupied for weeks getting his business set up in a new location, so their lack of contact was understandable. She still had feelings for him, but they were more friendly than romantic.

She had to admit that even though it made her feel weak, she was glad not to have to deal with that distraction any longer.

When she was dressed, she took a moment to affix the access device to Aza's back with a band that wrapped around his belly. At his smallest size, as big as a large crow, the device was almost as long as his torso and as wide as his body. He tested his wings to make sure he could still fly properly and flapped toward the ceiling, then landed on her shoulder like a pirate's parrot. She said with a laugh, "Arr, matey. Let's get a move on."

Cait opened a portal and stepped through. Aza flew off her shoulder toward the top of their target building. She summoned an autonomous vehicle and rode in the back for the couple of blocks to the building. She made a show of climbing out of it and smoothing her dress, then closed the door and went inside. A tuxedoed man approached her as she entered the lounge, but she waved him off and took a seat at the bar. The bartender from the previous evening came over and smiled. "I never forget a face. You were here last night but in a different outfit."

Cait laughed inwardly. The differences between the Lexi of the day before and the Lexi of today were far greater than the clothes. Her assessment before she left the apartment was that she was on the fringes of bombshell territory. She replied, "Very true. Last night, I was just sort of looking around after work."

He asked what she'd like, and she ordered a martini. As he made it in front of her, he asked, "So, what do you do?"

"Talent agent. I represent up-and-coming celebrities."

He looked up with a smile. "Really? I don't think I've ever met anyone in that business before."

She gave a small laugh since it was expected. "Well, it's a rarefied trade, that's for sure."

"Anyone I know?"

"Bethany Crisis."

His smile became a grin, and he seemed to be interested in her for the first time. "The punk band? That's fantastic. Is Bethany as cool as she seems?"

Cait rolled her eyes. "That girl is a world of trouble."

"So, that's a yes."

She grinned and accepted her drink. "Definitely." She made a mental note to have Sabrina find out more about the band in case she needed to use that alibi again. It had come to her in a flash, and she'd gone with it. The bartender departed, and she swiveled in her chair to watch the lobby while she sipped her drink. It took twenty-five minutes, but finally, all three men from the picture walked through her line of sight, going outside. She whispered, "They're out. Your guess on the timing was right."

Sabrina replied in her ear, "Don't worry, I'll say it for you. I'm the best."

Cait sent, *Aza, do your thing.*

---

Aza had listened to the conversations through his connection with Cait. She'd learned to echo everything she heard to him, and now it took an act of will for her not to share things. He launched himself into the air from an adjacent building and flapped hard to climb to the top of the target skyscraper. Sabrina had looked for plans of the place, and while she hadn't been able to find any for the building itself, she had discovered the name of the construction company and pulled diagrams of a different building they'd built with similar stuff on the roof.

The HVAC system was fed from a wide pipe, and panels in the apartments accessed the same channel. He flew to the grate, grabbed it in his claws, and flapped his wings hard. The bolts holding it sheared off and he flew backward, flapping again to halt his momentum. He dropped the screen and headed inside. The interior space didn't provide enough room to fly, so he braced himself with his claws on one side of the channel and his neck on the other and slowly walked downward, wedged between the sides.

Small pulses emerged from the device on his back, a code from Sabrina. A short vibration meant left. A long one, right. And the series of quick signals he'd just received told him to keep going straight. He guessed she was tracking his position with the thing on his back and maybe mapping the system of metal channels. He didn't fully understand what the woman did with her magic but knew that she was excellent at it.

The directions took him to a grate that looked out on a large room, positioned about a foot off the floor. The device vibrated with a triple-length signal, which told him to stop, and he complied. Cait echoed the infomancer's message to him. *Sabrina says she's found cameras and infrared sensors. She's working on defeating them.*

He replied, *I guess I'm not close enough to access anything fun?*

*Who knows. Only Sabrina understands the reason Sabrina does things.* After a few moments, the repeated pulses telling him to continue came out of the box. He pushed his body forward against the grate, which caused it to separate from the wall enough that he could see the screw on one side. A quick slash of his claw cut through it, and he pushed the barrier forward and down to give him room to move. Cait sent, *Sabrina says the defenses are nullified. See if you can find a phone or a computer or something.*

Aza jumped up and flew around the penthouse. He

checked the living room and dining room first since he'd emerged into the former and the latter was connected to it. The apartment was spotless, with not a thing out of place, which he thought would be an incredibly annoying way to live. He checked the kitchen next, then made his way into the bedroom. It had a desk, and on the desk was a laptop computer.

He landed beside it, put one claw on the top and the other on the bottom, and separated the pieces until it activated. The hold signal from Sabrina was immediate. He waited, wondering what was going on, until Cait sent, *Oh, hell. He's back. Aza, get out of there.*

---

Cait abruptly stood, holding her third drink in her hand, and allowed herself to wobble a bit as she walked. She headed for the door into the lobby and arrived a few steps behind the trio of men who'd just passed through the outer door. When she got close, she giggled and said, too loudly, "Zee. I haven't seen you for *so* long."

Her path was unsteady as she closed on the men, who had all turned to look at her. One's eyes were amused, but the other men glared, revealing who was in charge and who was security. She took another drink as she crossed the distance separating them and said, "Surely you remember me. From the lobby bar a couple months ago?" She stuck out her hand, and he took it, squeezing it gently.

His English was cultured and had a trace of a British accent. "I'm sorry, I don't remember. I'm sure that, had I spoken to someone as beautiful as you, I would not have forgotten it."

Cait put on a pout. "I'm sure it was you. Well, almost sure. I'd had a drink or two."

"I assure you, it wasn't me." He released her hand and turned away.

She called after them, "Sorry for bothering you. If you'd like to have a drink sometime, I'm here often. Just let me know."

He didn't reply but walked to the center elevator and was lost to sight as the doors closed. Aza reported, *I'm out,* and Cait turned to weave her way back to the lounge. She finished her drink at the bar while looking increasingly depressed over the scene she'd just made, then left, visibly defeated. *I sure hope Sabrina found something worth this little act of humiliation.*

## CHAPTER TEN

Carl Winston stepped out of the shower and rubbed his hand over his freshly shaven face. He'd spent several days in private mourning after Cynthia's death, but now he was over the emotional upheaval. He'd ventured out over the last couple of days to check on his people and was mildly alarmed at what he saw. Something seemed to have been lost among the Thorns' street-level people, maybe trust in their leadership, maybe confidence in themselves. He couldn't tell, but it called for action, so he needed to get his act together.

He dressed carefully, first slipping on his combat suit as he now did when leaving the bunker. He pulled on street clothes to hide it, and the only visible sign that he was geared up was the heavy boots that were more substantial than his normal wear. He had two guns, several blades, and an emergency equipment pack on him, plus healing and energy potions. He checked the mirror and verified that his untucked dress shirt hid everything adequately.

Carl opened a portal to the landing room in the warehouse but paused before stepping through. He stared hard at everything on the other side of the rift and used his magical senses to probe the area. Discovering no dangers, he stepped through and let the portal close. He unlocked the three deadbolts, opened the door, and crossed the threshold. After pulling the door closed, he used his magic to secure each lock again. Only then did he unlock the only other door into that room and pass through onto the warehouse floor.

When they'd made this their temporary base of operations, his people had moved the pallets of stored goods off to the sides to create an open center. His top soldiers were gathered around a beat-up metal table, each with papers or a computer in front of him or her. He took the empty seat at the head of the table and said, "All right. Report."

The subordinate who controlled the money was the first to speak. The man was the definition of bookish, and Carl guessed he'd been an accountant before deciding to join the criminal enterprise. "Money is down. My estimate is thirty percent, although since we don't have all our processes restored after the, uh, unfortunate incident, that's not a final number."

"Why are we down?"

One of his street enforcers, a man with a nose that had obviously been broken a few times and a small scar on his cheek, answered, "People are holding back on payments. I think they're not taking us as seriously as they should. Probably heard we're momentarily vulnerable and are trying to use that to their advantage."

Carl nodded. He'd expected that response. He'd seen it happen before, in fact, when the Roses had become the

Thorns. "I want you to think of some options for fixing that, but bloodless ones. What we can't do right now is afford to inspire more action against us." He shifted his gaze to another of his people. "Tell me what you found out about Huff."

The infomancer sniffed. He liked a little hit of recreational drugs before doing his runs, which Carl didn't love, but the man was competent enough that he was willing to accept the flaw. *For the moment, anyway.* The man's voice trembled when he said, "We've confirmed his known address is the real one where he spends most of his time. It's at the top of a building that a corporation he runs owns and is heavily guarded. So far, we've had no success at compromising his computer systems."

Carl nodded. "Keep on it. Other options?"

The short man with a long beard at the other end of the table laughed. His voice was hoarse as he suggested, "Drop the building."

He raised an eyebrow at his demolition expert, who had been a specialist in the military before opting for more lucrative options. "What a shock that that's your first suggestion." Everyone joined in the good-natured laughter. "Can you do it cleanly without collateral damage to the area or the buildings around it?"

The other man scratched his chin. "Only with time and access that we probably can't manage. So, no."

Carl nodded. "All right. We'll call that our last resort, then. Go ahead and figure out the best way to do it and lay in the supplies. If we don't use them for this project, I'm sure we'll be able to find another."

The lone woman at the table, one of his most skilled

subordinates and an expert in intelligence and planning, said, "We could hit him in transit. He uses decoy vehicles, though, so we'd have to strike them all simultaneously."

He frowned, having been excited about the idea before she revealed that caveat. "How many?"

She raised a hand in a helpless gesture. "Three to five. There doesn't seem to be a specific pattern or situation that inspires the choice of how many roll out."

His frown deepened. "Why doesn't he just have a magical portal him around?"

She replied, "His people need to see him out and about. Just like yours do, boss."

*Yeah. That's what got Cynthia killed.* "Could the person in the car be a double? And he himself travels differently?"

His intelligence specialist leaned forward. "You know, I never thought of that. I'd say it's quite possible. It's not as if it would be hard, especially if one of the guards with the double was a magical who could open a portal back to a secure location."

Carl nodded. "With enough money and the right motivation, you can accomplish all sorts of things. We're going to have to get creative."

His demolitions expert laughed. "What do you have in mind, boss?"

Carl stood and began to pace. "We'll work the problem from three directions." He looked at his money man. "First, have one of our clean businesses rent space in his building. Make sure the cover is airtight." The man nodded, and he continued, "Once we're in, we figure out how to spy on everyone else in the building."

The infomancer replied, "Love it."

Energy built inside Carl, something he hadn't felt in any abundance since Cynthia had died. It was like the Syndicate training said, action healed and overthinking poisoned. "Second, find out how he recruits for his businesses, his gang, his servants, and his local security. If there's a crack through which we can slip someone close to him, I want to know about it. No direct action without my go-ahead, but prepare the field." Murmurs of assent circled the table.

Carl grinned. "Finally, the honeypot. Find the most beautiful woman we have who's willing to take on the project and get her ready. She needs to know everything about Huff that we know, and we need to figure out the right place to put the two of them together."

The only woman in the room remarked, "Could be dangerous."

"Agreed, so make sure she's resourceful and figure out how she can smuggle in weapons to take care of Huff." He stopped pacing and turned to them. "Questions?" There were none. "Okay, get to it."

Carl portaled back to his bunker and laid down on the most comfortable couch. He closed his eyes and let his mind wander, and it showed him a vision of himself standing over Victor Huff's body, laughing as the light faded from his enemy's eyes. Out loud, he said, "Soon, Victor. You'll pay for sending your goons to kill Cynthia with your money, your organization, and your life. Once you're dead, everything you've built will be mine, and the world will forget you ever existed."

# CHAPTER ELEVEN

Sabrina emerged from the changing room in her workspace at the Moakley, ready for battle. She had on her oldest pair of combat boots with leather pants tucked into them. Her t-shirt displayed the cover of an album by the band Joy Division, which had ended in a fashion appropriate to their music with the untimely death of their lead singer.

Her makeup was dramatic. Full black around her eyes, bright red lips, and slashes of crimson on her cheeks. Her hair was bound in a topknot that let it spill out in all directions like a goth fountain. She pushed strands out of her face as she dropped into the chair in front of her computers. Her standard diagnostic resulted in all greens, meaning her hardware was ready to go.

She took the next several minutes to customize the avatar she'd use when she reached the enemy server, a samurai like the ones she'd seen on her last visit. Male, of course, since female samurai were not a thing at that moment in history. Armor in dull scarlet, with muted gold around the edges, an homage to the colors of the castle dampened with appropriate martial gravity.

A curved samurai sword was sheathed at her waist on the left side, angling backward from the armored skirt that touched her shins. The boots under covered her knees with metal. The similarities to real samurai armor were only visual, however. Her gear was programmed as if it were composed of modern materials, including carbon fiber, ballistic weave, and other refinements to make it resistant to all forms of damage.

Bandoliers holding small darts, each tipped with a poison that would immobilize her enemies instantly, then kill them over time, crossed her chest. A tube was attached to her left forearm, the gear's only obvious anachronism. The bolt launcher fired sharpened projectiles on a burst of gunpowder. It was auto-fed and carried five shots, one in the barrel and four reloads. Her belt held a variety of other tricks and gadgets appropriate to the simulation.

When she was satisfied that her preparations were as complete as she could make them, Sabrina threw herself into the data stream and rode it to the castle. Her avatar materialized inside the outer perimeter created by the dragons' patrol. She lifted the helmet from under her arm and fastened it on her head, pulling the chin strap tight. *Just one more totally normal samurai. Nothing to see here.*

She walked forward with confidence but chose not to head straight for the front doors as she had before. Instead, she patrolled the compound and carefully examined each of the outbuildings as she passed it. She judged that the first structure she came to was a barracks. The other, its mirror image, she identified as a recreational space for off-duty guards. It was more or less what she'd expected to find since things like kitchens and food storage would be inside the castle in case of attack.

Sabrina continued her wandering and concentrated on looking as if she had a purpose. She found a side entrance guarded by a single samurai and had to keep herself from smiling. Instead, she stopped moving and stared expectantly at the door. Her deception programs launched an assault against his recognition system, and after several moments, she won. The guard stepped aside, and she walked past him.

Beyond the door was a service hallway, and she turned right toward the back of the building. She heard the faint noises she'd expected and followed them into the kitchen, the center of gossip for any community. She stood in the doorway, watching and listening. Eventually, an older woman stopped, laughed at her, and spoke. Although her mouth formed words that weren't in English, Sabrina's ears received them in her own language.

"Young soldiers. Always hungry." She made a clucking noise with her tongue and slipped a rice cake to Sabrina. She thanked her with a smile and continued listening. It required twenty minutes of loitering before she had the information she needed. The leader would be eating in his room that evening, and someone would have to deliver it to the fourth floor. *Now I know where to go. Of course it's the top level.*

She marveled that the simulation was so accurate and detailed. It didn't require a lot of processing power to emulate the operations of such a place, but still, it was impressively done. She felt a kinship with the designer because when she built defensive emplacements, she did the same. Details mattered.

*That means I'll find guard patrols and possibly traps, and there's likely no easy way to sneak up there.* Sabrina sauntered toward the front of the building and emerged from the service corridor into the main area. The space appeared to be a reception hall, with no furniture in the expanse and lights and paintings on the walls. It rose two stories in the middle, with the outer area having less height because of the second-floor balcony. That level had several guarded doors that doubtless led to inner rooms.

A narrow staircase on the opposite side of the room from the service corridor led to the second floor, and she nodded at the pair of samurai guarding it as she passed. She'd already established her credentials with first-floor security, and they made no move to stop her. She assumed she would need to win that battle again on every level, as each likely represented increasing protection for the leader. The ease with which she'd breached the outer defenses pleased her, and she was confident she would be able to handle whatever awaited her on the second floor.

When she emerged on the balcony, she nodded in appreciation at the design of the simulation. Several of the doorways along the periphery were guarded by samurai, and she couldn't access the route to the third floor without passing every one of them. The floor was quiet as if whatever people did in this place, they did it behind closed doors and tried not to be heard.

Sabrina strolled toward the first guard and launched her deception programs. She monitored the battle as they fought the security system and deployed an additional attack by reaching out and touching the samurai on the shoulder. He stiffened at the contact, then relaxed. She inclined her head in acknowledgment and continued forward to receive a small smile from the next samurai in line. *I'm clear here, but I don't think I'll get away with that tactic again.*

Maintaining her cover had required deploying one of her stronger programs, and while she had others in reserve that worked in different ways, they weren't inherently more powerful. She made a left-hand turn to walk along the upper level at the front of the building, then took another left to head to the only door that wasn't on the outer wall. She was sure it blocked the stairs to the next level and equally positive that the samurai guarding it would present a greater challenge than the others had.

Sabrina triggered a set of bots she'd prepared earlier and quickened her steps toward the guardian of the staircase. Outside, a small group of bandits on horseback would emerge from the fields where she'd deployed her programs and charge for the front door. Shouts of alarm came from below. Though the floor's other guards rushed down the stairs, the one in front of her didn't move, confirming that he was a higher-level challenge than they were.

The samurai started to draw his sword as she neared him, but she was faster. She grabbed a dart out of her bandolier, stepped inside his guard, and rammed it up through his chin from underneath. He stiffened as the poison did its work, and she reached around him to grab the door handle behind him. It was locked, and she shoved her body against his to hold him up while her programs worked on the lock.

In the virtual world, she searched the samurai and found the key that allowed her to open the door. His body fell through, and she lifted his legs and shut the door behind her. She locked it again and slipped the key into her pouch, then waited to see if she'd set off any other alarms. None sounded. A quick search of her foe revealed that he carried two slim knives, and she jammed them into the seam between the door and the frame to further barricade it.

The other staircases had involved switchbacks, but this one didn't. It led to a landing with a door. Unfortunately, that door was a couple of feet from the stairs, so she didn't see the samurai guarding it until she was upon him.

Sabrina reacted in an instant as he opened his mouth to shout. Her left arm rose to the proper angle and caressed the bolt-launcher's firing stud. With a loud pop, a bolt crossed the foot of space between them and took him in the throat. His hand scrabbled at it for a moment while he stared at her without understanding, then he fell.

She moved his body aside and peered through the keyhole. She'd hoped to see a matching door across the way that indicated the staircase to the fourth floor and the leader who hung out there, but whoever had designed the place was smarter than that. Her view was limited to profiles of a pair of samurai guards standing nearby. She paused to listen and heard the footsteps of others patrolling. *A drone would be really handy here. Or maybe x-ray glasses, like in the old comic books.* Laughing at herself, Sabrina opened the door with the key she'd stolen and charged through it.

# CHAPTER TWELVE

As Sabrina's samurai avatar ran through the door, her hand dropped to the hilt of her sword. By the time she reached the pair of guards standing idly against the wall, who were just beginning to react to her presence, it was halfway from its sheath. The draw and strike were a single movement as her weapon slashed their throats an inch above their armor.

Their faces filled with panic as they collapsed. Had they been other than computer representations of artificial intelligences, she might have found the scene disturbing. She'd played enough gory video games that it didn't affect her, and besides, her mind was moving far too fast to worry about such things. She spun and flicked her sword out in a wide arc, both to clear the blood from it and to intercept any attacks coming at her. None were since her sudden appearance had surprised the defenders.

Seven enemies were present in her field of view, which encompassed the whole floor. Couches and other furniture were arranged around the periphery, but the center was empty, aside from the samurai. Sabrina imagined it as a performance space, where the actors would occupy the middle while aristocrats lounged along the sides, and again felt a kinship with the designer's choices. At the moment, though, the only show would involve blades, blood, and figurative death.

The leftmost one grabbed a bow from the chair beside him and nocked an arrow. The projectile was flying toward her before she had time to process his attack. Fortunately for her, the samurai was an artificial intelligence. As an infomancer, her magically powered reflexes were faster than any bot. She reached out with her left hand and snagged the arrow from the air half a foot from her face.

Sabrina hurled it at another of the samurai as a distraction, then leveled her left arm at the archer and fired a bolt at him. It missed but forced him to evade, which eliminated him as an immediate threat. The boldest of the defenders rushed her from the right. She skipped back to avoid his thrust, whipped her blade down in a two-handed curving block to knock his weapon aside, and stepped in as her circle rose. Her advance drove her steel through the samurai's throat.

As she pulled it out, she fired a bolt and took out another of the samurai. Four were down, and five remained. The nearest moved faster than expected, and she let her left leg collapse and rolled out of the way. Sabrina came up with her sword in her left hand and used it to block a slash from another samurai. Her right hand flicked out twice, sending poison darts at nearby targets. One struck true, cutting into a cheek, but the other hit armor and fell away. *Four left.*

She flinched aside in the nick of time to cause the archer's second arrow to stab into her armor instead of her neck. It caught her in the shoulder, and while it failed to penetrate, the power of the blow hurt. Sabrina pushed the sensation away with a frown. She'd detected a difference in her remaining enemies. Two moved with greater assurance and speed than the others. *Infomancers.*

She charged the archer and cut him down before he could get his blade free to defend himself. Another bolt from her forearm took out the other program. She turned to face the remaining pair, who stood in the center of the room with the flats of their swords resting on their shoulders, watching. The two were identical in all respects. The first said, "Well done. You massacred some bots. You must feel very good about yourself."

Sabrina copied their sword position. "You should hire better programmers."

The second laughed. "Oh, we have better programmers. They're currently tracing your location in the real world. When we find you, well, some of our people will stop by to have a long conversation with you about not breaking in where you don't belong."

Sabrina let out a condescending snort. "Listen, pal. The virus I seeded your system with isn't going to allow you to catch me or anyone else." It was a lie, but sowing doubt in one's enemies was always a good practice.

The one on the left shrugged. "We'll deal with that after we deal with you." They attacked simultaneously, moving away from each other to flank her. She grabbed a poison dart and hurled it at the one on the left side. He raised his sword to intercept, and she danced away to engage the one on the right.

His sword came down in a diagonal slash at her shoulder, and she whipped hers up to block and carry the strike out the side. She snapped a kick into the samurai guard's groin, which turned out to be appropriately armored. A quick backpedal took her out of danger as he brought his sword across to clash with hers again, and she moved right to keep him between her and the other one. Her left arm rose, and she fired her fourth bolt.

The samurai in front of her dodged, but the one behind him failed to. It struck him in the shoulder and pierced his armor. She snarled because she'd hit him in his off-hand, and he gritted his teeth, growled a curse, and rushed her. Sabrina ran away and sprinted to the far side of the room while waving her sword behind her to deflect whatever attacks might come. She slammed another program into action when she reached the wall and ran up it, ending up running upside-down on the ceiling.

Her intervention in the simulation's physics wouldn't last long, but she didn't need much time. She crossed directly over her opponents, who weren't quick enough to bring their swords up to catch her. Her sword slashed the one with the bolt in his shoulder across the side of the neck. Blood spurted, and he slapped a hand to the gash, then went down.

Her negation of gravity failed, and she fell. Sabrina landed awkwardly on her side and rolled immediately, narrowly avoiding being punctured by the sword that struck the wooden floor at her back. She rose to face the remaining enemy infomancer. He shifted his blade to a high guard, then bellowed and charged. She deflected his blows, which came in at a challenging rate. His strength was equal to hers, and his speed was possibly greater.

They marched back and forth across the room, exchanging strikes. Realizing that the impasse would likely continue as long as he and she were both careful, she dodged a blow instead of blocking and reached for the pouch at her belt. She extracted a smoke bomb and slammed it on the floor. It exploded with incandescent brilliance, and her enemy staggered back.

In the real world, she'd launched a hack to overload his video feed and white out his view. He was unable to see for only a moment, but when his vision returned, her sword had been shoved through his chest to the hilt. Blood trickled from his mouth as he gasped, "Dirty trick," then slid off her blade to the floor. She flicked the blade clean and moved to the staircase on the other side. Time was critical now that she was known to the enemy infomancers. She rushed up the stairs, which turned twice, and rammed her shoulder into the door at the top. It slammed open, and she raised her sword two-handed to block.

The man sitting in the luxurious-looking wingback chair closed his book and set it on the nearby table. He was dressed in fine silk garments, loose-fitting trousers, and an embroidered tunic, and his feet were bare. His dark hair fell around his shoulders, and his face was nondescript, as if he could have been any forty-something man. He said in a cultured voice, "Welcome."

Sabrina's gaze searched the rest of the chamber for potential dangers. It appeared to be part of a suite of rooms. A buffet table with fresh fruit stood on one side, across from glass shelves that displayed premium spirits. A couch occupied the back of the space, and a second chair was positioned next to the one he occupied. He smiled. "You're not one of mine. Good disguise, though. Security failure is far preferable to treachery."

Sabrina frowned and returned her eyes to him. "One of yours? Who are you?" She guessed he was the chief infomancer and flexed her hands on her sword's hilt.

He laughed. "I am the Cui Siwang."

"Like, *the* Cui Siwang?"

His eyes registered mirth. "You didn't do your research before braving my castle?"

She scowled. "There's nothing out there about you being an infomancer."

He rose from his chair and brushed his clothes to smooth them. "Infomancy, like other magics, can be learned. Doubtless, if we met on neutral ground, I would have no chance against you." His voice hardened slightly. "But here, it should be a fair fight, and while we battle, my systems and people will find your flesh. Shortly after that, you will receive a visit from my soldiers."

Sabrina ignored the threat. "Why learn infomancy?"

He raised an eyebrow. "Perhaps it's so natural to you that you don't realize how amazing this place is. Being here gives one time to think. In this space, at the speed of data, I can properly reflect before making decisions."

"Okay, enough talk." She rushed forward and slashed her blade at his neck, hoping for a quick kill. He side-stepped with unexpected speed and used his palm to push the flat of her sword past him. A deft dip and twist preceded his hard shot to her kidney. It struck her armor and failed to penetrate, although the strike landed harder than she'd expected it would.

He landed another blow on the back of her leg as she was twisting. It compromised her horizontal slice and sent it up past his head. He flowed in and used his right arm to grab her wrist and yank the limb out straight. His next move would've been to shatter her elbow, but she dove forward, surrendering the sword to break his grip. She shoulder-rolled, came up with a poison dart in her hand, and whipped it at him.

He deflected it with her sword. *Rude*. He seemed uncomfortable with the weapon and used it like a baseball bat to take wild swings at her. The length of the blade and his arms kept her from an easy counterattack. She circled, looking for a way in, and reached for another poison dart, only to find she'd used them all. He slashed again, and she leaned back to avoid it, then tried a backspin to kick his feet out from under him.

He took a few steps back, laughed, and waved the sword in a flashy figure eight. "I think you are in trouble, invader." He paced forward confidently, the blade raised high to cut her down. Sabrina stood, lifted her right hand to distract him, and angled her left down. The bolt shot out of the launcher and into his foot to pin it to the floor. He cried out in pain, and she circled quickly to get behind him while he was distracted. One punch to the temple dazed him, and the second rendered him unconscious.

She retrieved her sword, sheathed it, and headed for one of the doors that led out of the room. On the other side was an office with an old-style desk, a calligraphy brush and ink, and a large ledger. She grabbed the book and blinked in surprise as the world faded around her.

When she opened her eyes, she was in her office. The failsafe in DC had disconnected her from the Cui Siwang system. She checked to be sure she'd acquired data from the final room and confirmed that she had. Whatever the ledger held, it was now hers, assuming she could decode it. She shook her head. "Hell. That was close. This better have been worth it."

# CHAPTER THIRTEEN

Lady Rebecca Olanyr passed through the portal from the chill surroundings of her home into the cool evening of the woods in Ireland. She didn't anticipate trouble but, as always, she was prepared for it.

Silver weapons that would harm the lycanthropes if things got messy were hidden in her robes, and her magic was adequate to deal with almost any threat. She had little fear that the werewolves would attack. The worst case was that they would refuse to help her and abandon the partnership to remove the witches and retake their ancestral lands.

If that happened, it would upset her plans in an unacceptable way. It wouldn't deal them a fatal blow, but it would make things challenging that should be easy. Therefore, convincing them was important. Fortunately, she owned the heart, mind, and loyalty of the wolves' new leader, Luciana. She had supported the woman in her bid to lead the pack, and now, despite a culture that generally didn't follow females, she ruled them.

Rebecca figured the odds were even that one of the members of the pack would attempt to kill Luciana during the attack, which gave her a pang of regret. She liked the other woman and, more importantly, respected her commitment to achieving her goals. The plan was what mattered, though, and she couldn't concern herself with anything but its success.

She released her concealing veil as she stepped into the circle. The wolves did not start at her appearance, for which she gave them credit. Luciana nodded at her, then addressed the packs. "We have gathered tonight to review the final details of our attack against the witches. It has been a long path to this place. We have seen successes and failures along the way, but all that is behind us. We must focus everything we are on what lies ahead."

She moved as she spoke, pacing to keep their attention on her. "This battle, this chance to reclaim our territory, is the defining moment for our future. Success will unify our kind as never before. Other shifters will flock to the area, and we will be the ones holding the power. It is our destiny to do so. I've seen it in dreams that were like visions. Some of you that I've talked to have as well. We are on the cusp of greatness, and if we do not falter, it will be ours."

She turned to Rebecca. The wolf leader had worn clothes, which Rebecca was thankful for. About half of the other wolves had done the same, but the rest were naked, a situation they were clearly comfortable with. "Lady Olanyr will explain the plan we've worked out together."

Rebecca stepped forward with a smile. In truth, it was *her* plan, and Luciana had agreed to it since she'd had no other option. The wolves' leader had made a couple of suggestions that Rebecca had integrated into her strategy, but nothing pivotal. She raised her voice. "You all know me or know of me. The moment has come for us to fulfill our promises to one another. Two nights from now, the moon will be full. I cannot think of a more appropriate time to bring this business to a close. I will be there to support your attack, and together, we shall reclaim your land."

Her words set off a cascade of conversation among the wolves, some of it sounding eager but not all. An undercurrent of resistance ran through several small groups. Luciana shouted, "Pay attention. Time is short, and we have much to accomplish. We *will* do this. Anyone who has reservations is free to leave their pack."

Her harsh words looked to have taken them by surprise, and a few exchanged glances. Rebecca thought they might move, but they didn't. When they'd settled again, she continued, "The attack has three parts. Each is of vital importance. Luciana will choose who participates in which. That is not my concern. I will be with you at the start of each fight and transport you to the location so we can achieve surprise."

Her audience's confidence grew. She saw it in their expressions and the way they subtly shifted to face her. "We will start with an attack on Westport." The comment was well-received. The wolves had enjoyed success in the town before, and parts of the group harbored an intense hatred of the people who lived there.

"It will not be our primary target, however. Its purpose is to draw off protectors from the witches' village. Once they show up to join in the defense, we will avoid getting caught up in a direct engagement. Should that prove difficult, we'll fall back to the woods and attempt to keep them busy."

A male shouted, "And if they only respond with a small number?"

Rebecca grinned. "If you have the numerical advantage, by all means, kill them. However, it's my estimation that they will come in modest force at a minimum. Our goal is to sow chaos and make ourselves seem more dangerous than we are to draw more people to the town. I will assist with that." She offered a grin that showed her canines. "Fire is always good for striking fear into the populace."

That statement earned her positive murmurs. "Once that is complete, another group will attack the coven. What we've done before has worked, so we will do the same thing again. We gather in force and engage from all directions, targeting the weak and vulnerable first. This battle needs to last longer than the one in Westport. Again, if defeat seems imminent, the plan is to break away and fade because the goal is not the village."

A female called, "Then what is it?"

The exasperation in her tone made Rebecca laugh inside. "Our objective is Croagh Patrick. It is the source of this place's magical power and acts as a protector. The witches are strengthened by it. Defeating them while it remains in their hands will be virtually impossible." Her words were a patchwork of lies. Yes, it was powerful, but it wasn't part of the witches' strength. The wolves didn't need to know that, and they did need to be committed to taking the mountain, which was *her* objective.

"When the battle is underway and most of the witches have joined the fight, a group will portal to the base of the mountain. I can't get us any higher since the place is closed to my power. It has a guardian, and though he is weakening, he has identified me as his enemy and will act against my efforts."

The first man who'd spoken asked, "How is that not a recipe for failure?"

Rebecca offered him a confident smile. "If you can get me to the top safely, I can break his power and cut off his support of the witches. When he calls them for help, which he will, we must have them too occupied to immediately come to his aid. *That* is how we'll succeed.

"Once we reach the top, I will claim the mountain's power. When I do, I'll be able to influence the surrounding lands. The witches' strength will be weakened, and then we will attack them again with everything we have. They will flee or die. The same is true of the people in Westport. When the sun rises on Sunday, my friends, the mountain will belong to me, the surrounding lands will belong to you, and all will thrive under my protection."

She didn't see who howled in approval first, but shortly thereafter, all the wolves, both in human and lupine form, were baying their agreement.

# CHAPTER FOURTEEN

Cait had forgotten that this was to be a special day at the office, so when she walked in and saw the balloons and decorations that filled the room, her mind went into vapor lock for a moment. From where she stood on a chair, attaching a streamer to the ceiling, Sabrina laughed down at her. "You look like you just wandered into the twilight zone. You okay, Cait?"

She shook her head. "Yeah, I'm fine. I forgot about this, so it came as a bit of a surprise."

The infomancer climbed down and walked over to her. "Then I guess you probably forgot it was your job to pick up the cake at the bakery?"

Cait replied, "*Damn*. True. Totally forgot."

Sabrina grinned. "I guess it's good you can do that magic portal thing, huh? Go, and don't come back without baked goods."

"Sir, yes, sir."

The other woman laughed. "Maybe bring me an extra

cinnamon roll for the inconvenience of me having to remind you of your job."

Cait grinned. "You drive a hard bargain, lady. I'll be back." She headed to the courtyard to escape the building's anti-magic field and portaled to a spot she knew near the bakery. It left her with a few blocks to walk, but it was a sunny and temperate day, so she didn't mind the requirement. She felt a little guilty at the realization that she hadn't thought about Simon Levitt, the former chief of her office, in a while. Things had been busy, and he'd been out of danger and had vanished from her thoughts. *Well, that's something I can try to keep from happening again. Lesson learned.*

She retrieved the cake and portaled back. Sabrina demanded in a dire tone, "Cinnamon roll?"

Cait laughed and fished the small bag out of her purse. "Here you go, O great one."

Her friend smirked. "And don't you forget it."

Arranging the security clearances for the guests took the rest of the morning, and at lunchtime, everyone arrived. They'd brought in catered sandwiches and had soda, tea, and champagne for everyone, plus the cake, of course. Before any of that could be touched, though, Susan demanded that their prior chief say a few words.

Simon looked good despite the grievous injuries he'd taken during the unprovoked attack on the marshals. He walked with a cane, but his skin tone looked healthy, and his expression seemed freer and happier than she'd ever seen him be. She nudged Sabrina. "Seems like retirement suits him well."

Sabrina replied, "Him and his wife both. She looks radiant." It was true. Nicole appeared decades younger than she had when faced with the terror of her husband's injuries. As a pair, they looked calm and joyful, and it warmed Cait's heart to see it.

Simon cleared his throat. "Thank you all for coming. If I'd realized how many people I'd annoyed enough that they'd want to be here to see me finally go away, I might not have done this just to deny you all the closure." The crowd laughed.

"Seriously, thank you all for being here. I miss you. I miss *this*." He waved around the office. "If you told me a month before I was injured that I would find comfort in retirement, I wouldn't have believed you, but truly, this is a good time for me to leave. Susan is a more than adequate replacement to lead this office."

Garrett called, "Improvement."

Everyone laughed, and Simon pointed a finger at him. "Behave, or I'll hit you with my cane." That generated more laughter. He continued, "If anyone wants to meet me for a round of golf sometime, just let me know." He finished with specific words for specific people, then the crowd dove into the food and broke up into small conversational circles.

Cait stopped to speak with him and his wife, saying the sorts of innocuous things one said at such a time. She'd told the chief what he meant to her before, and she was confident he remembered. She gravitated toward the edge of the room and watched the happy people celebrating.

Sabrina came over with an overly large piece of cake and stood beside her. "This is good. He deserves to have some calm and happiness in his life."

Cait chuckled. "So do we all. Unfortunately, that's not our fate just yet."

Sabrina commented, "Speaking of which, I did another run against the Cui Siwang servers."

Cait coughed on her champagne, then wiped her mouth and glared at her friend. "You just throw that out. Like, with no warning. You're a damned maniac."

Sabrina laughed. "If I'd told you ahead of time, you would've worried. No point in that."

"Did you learn anything useful?"

"Oh, yeah. I really did. You'll probably want to have a conversation with your friend Yoshino real soon."

Cait agreed after hearing the news and requested to meet with Yoshino. The other woman wasn't available until dinnertime, so they met after work at a downtown steakhouse. It was an exclusive place, but Cait still felt strange being out with the Dragons' leader in a public area. They made small talk while perusing the menu. Cait ordered wild-caught salmon, and her companion did the same. Aza muttered in her head about his sadly unfulfilled desire for wild-caught salmon, and she promised they'd find him some as soon as the meal was over.

The other thing that was odd about the meeting was that Yoshino didn't look like herself. Cait had grown accustomed to seeing her in her Dragons finery, which was markedly different from the black pinstripe business suit and black blouse she currently wore. Her makeup was minimal, and only the way her hair was piled up and secured with ivory chopstick-style hairpins brought her traditional garb to mind. Cait asked, "Why are you dressed down today?"

Yoshino chuckled. "Only someone who knows how I usually look would consider this very expensive suit dressing down. I spent the afternoon at a board meeting for one of our companies. The other directors prefer not to be reminded that they are part of the Dragons."

Cait frowned and paused in dissecting her wedge salad. "You permit that?"

Her companion shrugged. "The company is only a means to an end. It has no value to me beyond that. They may feel and think what they like as long as what I need to have happen happens."

"What end is that?"

Yoshino plucked at a piece of lettuce with her scarlet fingernails, brought it to her lips, chewed, and swallowed. "Making the Dragons part of the foundation of this city. The more we diversify, the more influence we have, and the better we safeguard our survival."

Cait nodded. It tracked with what she knew of the woman and her priorities. "Speaking of survival, it appears that the Cui Siwang intend to eliminate the leaders of all the gangs in Boston, big and small."

Her companion remained calm and sounded unconcerned when she asked, "How did you come by this information?"

"An infomancer hacked their system."

Yoshino nodded. "She's very good. Your office infomancer. Sabrina Morin, I believe?"

Quiet alarm bells rang in Cait's head. "Yes. She's incredibly skilled and my close friend."

Yoshino's expression turned serious. "Your tone suggests you think I might have reason to harm your friend. The oath I swore to you precludes me from harming those you care about as well. I couldn't be true to you while hurting your family, whether linked by blood or choice."

The words reassured her, and Cait laughed as she thought about the big picture. "This is all so strange. You're a criminal. You've killed people."

"As have you."

Cait countered, "For the right reasons."

Yoshino spread her hands, palms up. "I believe the same."

Cait stabbed her fork into her lettuce with a laugh. "I give up. I hope the day never comes that we have to sort this out."

The waiter chose that moment to deliver their main dishes. When he was gone, Yoshino said, "As do I, Marshal Keane. As do I."

Cait watched her wield her knife to deftly cut apart the fish on her plate and remembered Paul's comment about the other woman being good with a sword. *If that day comes, following Simon into retirement might be the smarter choice.*

# CHAPTER FIFTEEN

After the busy week, Cait was more than ready to return to her family's home and relax. She arrived in time to help with breakfast, and during the meal, she said she and Aza would be heading to Oriceran to visit the dragons. It was a black mark against her in her mind that they hadn't done so sooner, given that the last time they'd seen them had been in the aftermath of the huge battle against the shadow creatures.

Brianna and Aisling immediately piped up that they would come along. Her father made a show of considering it, even though she knew he would join them, and finally said, "I think the coven's defenses can spare me for an afternoon."

Her mother, at the opposite end of the table, waved his concern away. "We've got the routine down now. Go. Have fun. Say hello for me. Don't be too late. You all have obligations this afternoon."

Cait replied, "I don't."

Her mother smiled. "Yes, you do. You're helping me with dinner."

Brianna shouted, "Score," and threw a napkin that struck Cait in the face. She flicked her fingers and spilled Brianna's coffee into her lap.

Her sister shot up, ready to dive across the table and tackle her, she was sure, but her mother snapped, "Children."

Cait laughed. "We'll wait for you to change before we go."

Brianna shot her a dirty look but couldn't hide her amusement and headed upstairs. Cait followed and changed into hiking boots, cargo pants, and a loose long-sleeve dress shirt over a tank top. She wasn't sure, what with the temperature would be on Oriceran, and the outfit gave her options. A gesture brought her shillelagh to her hand, and she went outside.

Aza was waiting in the small front yard. She felt his excitement through their connection and chided herself again for the delay. Then she chided herself for being too critical.

Fortunately, the others arrived and cut off the spiral of stupidity in her head. She opened a portal to the spot near the mountain where she'd first met Aza. They walked the modest distance to the place where Aza's family hung out and were greeted by a raucous display of whirling dragons. Aza leapt into the air, increased his size to match theirs, and joined in as they wheeled around, chased one another, and played some sort of roughhouse dragon game.

Aza's parents, Coazzir and Issha, were lying in the grassy field, basking in the sun. Cait walked up to the elder dragon, whose head, resting on the ground, was taller than she was. *It's hard to believe the shadow creatures were a threat to something so massive and majestic.* She began, "You look well."

He snorted softly and spoke into her mind. *We are well. In large part, thanks to you.* His eyes shifted, and his mouth twitched into what she recognized as a smile. *And your family. Please tell them they are welcome and it is good to see them.*

She echoed the words. Her father asked, "Can I ask him some questions about the area?"

Cait laughed. "Later."

She explained to Coazzir what her father wanted, and the dragon chuffed. *He is a knowledge seeker. We are happy to share what we know.*

"Is the young dragon who was taken okay?"

Issha said, *He has bad memories, but fortunately, he was not treated poorly by the wizard beyond the abduction. He is fine or will be soon.*

She smiled as something inside her eased. Cait hadn't realized she'd still been concerned about the dragons, but that was the only explanation for what she felt. She stretched out a tentative hand to touch Coazzir, and when he didn't stop her, she placed it against a scale, marveling that her partner would someday be this large. She tentatively asked, "Aza would be accepted back if he wanted to return home, right?"

Issha replied, *Always and forever. His path is his to choose, but we support any decision he makes.*

"I hope you won't take it poorly that I'd like it if that time doesn't come soon."

Coazzir gave a rumbling chuckle. *Being with you makes Azasania very happy.*

The seriousness of the moment was shattered when Aisling ran up, grabbed Cait's arm, and said, "Ask if one of the other dragons wants to come with me."

Cait sighed and shared the request. Unfortunately for her sister, none of the dragons were interested in relocating. They spent a couple more hours with the dragons, during which her father quizzed them on the area while Cait served as interpreter. After saying their goodbyes and promising to come back before long, they portaled home.

The coven was unexpectedly active. Half the village was in the central area, arranged in a circle with space left in the middle. Cait walked up to her mother, who stood a couple of rows back, and saw that the coven's two most powerful fighters were having a bout. Sashura used magic exclusively, and Delsanra focused on weapons supplemented by magic. They fought at full intensity, each confident in their own ability. As a practical matter, each had healing potions at their sides, and the coven's healers were nearby.

The battle ended in a draw, as it usually did. Sashura called several members of the coven over, including Cait and Aisling. She organized them in a circle with her in the center. "All of you have been working with me on phased magics. It's time for you to see how competent the others have become." What Cait thought of as Sashura's "teacher smile," which radiated understanding, appeared on her face. "This is not an easy skill to master since it requires you to split your very mind."

She paused, then, with perfect comedic timing, added,

"The people who are not with us are incapable of holding on to more than one thought at a time." The comment was made with dry sarcasm, and laughter greeted it.

Aisling hissed, "That explains why Brianna's not here."

Before Cait could add an insult about their older sister, Sashura snapped, "Fire shield." Each witch in the circle snapped up the required defense. "Now add lightning." Cait did it with ease and was pleased to see that her sister managed it as well, although with slightly more effort. The concentration it required was visible on Aisling's face. *I guess constant experience assists with this sort of thing. Lucky me.*

Sashura took them through each possible combination of paired magics. By the end, a fourth of the group had fallen away, their power reserves exhausted, or because they had to leave to attend to other responsibilities.

To those who remained, Sashura said, "Emulate me." She summoned a shield of force, and everyone copied it. Another spell added lightning crackling around the edges, and Cait copied it with ease. Aisling needed a few extra seconds to manage it.

Sashura said, "The same principle applies to adding a third magic. Focus your mind and your will and give me lightning." Sashura's shield crackled with the new addition. Cait focused another part of her mind and brought the required element into her shield. Aisling accomplished it as well but could only sustain it for a few seconds before it fell away. Others in the circle had the same experience.

Sashura gave a wicked smile and said, "Now frost." Cait managed it, though it taxed her abilities. Only one other witch was still with them. Her teacher nodded and called,

"Shadow." The other witch let her spells drop since she hadn't trained in the magic, which left Sashura and Cait facing one another, fully shielded from any potential attack. Cait released the spell with a groan, and Sashura laughed. "You're not doing your exercises, Caitriona."

"Right. I hear you."

Sashura waved. "Go. Good work."

Cait showered to wake herself up, then helped her mother get dinner ready. After they'd finished their meal, Will knocked on the door. It didn't come as a surprise. He obviously had a good source telling him when she would be around. She figured the communication probably started with her mother, although Moira would doubtless never admit it. They held hands as they walked around the clearing and talked about innocuous things.

Finally, Cait said, "This is good. It's nice to be with you."

He smiled. "And with you. Same time tomorrow?"

She laughed. "You're asking for a lot of commitment."

He didn't turn to look at her, but his grin widened. "Think you're ready for it?"

She considered for a moment, then, with her own smile, replied, "Yeah. I think I am. Same time tomorrow."

# CHAPTER SIXTEEN

Lady Rebecca Olanyr vibrated with anticipation. Finally, the long road she'd walked would reach its end. She wore tight-fitting armor under long robes, with healing and energy potions aplenty at her belt. Her plan was to sip the energy potion at every lull in the action to maintain her full power for the final battle. She closed her eyes and focused inward, concentrated her breathing, and sharpened her attention on the task at hand. It required walling away her hopes for what would come after, but she managed it with difficulty.

When her eyes opened, she felt ready for whatever might occur and conjured a portal to the staging area. Seeing all the wolves in one place invigorated her further. Their numbers had grown more than she'd realized, despite the losses they'd taken.

She'd known Elstan had met with other packs to persuade them to join the cause but hadn't realized how successful that effort had been. In her mind, it had to have been his work; she couldn't imagine that the late and unlamented Kellam had done anything during his leadership, and Luciana hadn't had enough time to pull this many wolves together.

The wolves' new leader was the only one in human form. She was clad in a loose robe, and Rebecca nodded her appreciation of the choice. "You're ready?"

Luciana replied, "We are. The group on the far right is for Westport. The center group is for the coven. My pack, twenty-five strong, will attack the mountain."

Rebecca smiled. She'd anticipated Luciana would want to be there for the culmination of their partnership and was pleased to be proven correct. It was also good to know that the group she thought of as the most reliable pack would be at her side for that battle. "All right, then. Let's do it."

Luciana shouted, "First group. Move it."

Rebecca opened a portal to connect the gathering place to the outskirts of Westport and followed the wolves through. She struck the initial blow of the fight by hurling a series of fireballs at the closest buildings. The wolves attacked a moment later. They flooded forward and savaged the panicked citizens near their incursion point.

It had taken a great deal of convincing by Luciana to make them understand and accept that their goal was not to kill the town's inhabitants but to wound them and sow chaos. They'd been mollified by the promise that the killing would come after the witches responded. Once all the magicals were dead, they could finish off those mundane citizens who were too stupid to run away at leisure. She hurled another round of fireballs that set several buildings across the street ablaze, then retreated into the tree line, popped the cap on an energy potion, and sipped it. She'd wait and watch the rest of this battle, although if the opportunity to pick off one of the witches presented itself, she, like the wolves, might find it difficult to hold back from a fatal strike.

---

The coven's alert system thundered over the village. People raced from their homes to the center area, and Delsanra took command when he arrived, shouting orders to the assembled witches and wizards. "The wolves are attacking Westport. Primary defense group, let's go." A subset of those staying behind opened portals, and the defenders charged through.

Cait was part of the primary group but wasn't dressed for the occasion. She sent Aza ahead and ran up to her room. It only took a few minutes to don her armor and weapons, and she invested another one to slip on her gun belt. The pistol had fifteen shots plus an extra magazine on the belt. It didn't hold the silver bullets the legends claimed were necessary, but the anti-magic rounds in the gun would work on the wolves. She darted back out and rushed through the nearest portal.

It deposited her in the city's main square. Werewolves dashed in pursuit of fleeing citizens. She wanted to go after them immediately, but Delsanra had insisted they fight in pairs, which meant her primary goal was to find her partner. She called to Aza, *Where's Brianna?*

He replied, *One block in front of you.* She pumped magic into her muscles and dashed ahead at top speed, forcing herself to ignore the wolves along the way. Their ragtag arrival at the fight meant Brianna was fighting alone, although Aza had watched over her in Cait's absence. They'd drilled on this routine every weekend, so it seemed the most normal thing in the world to run to her sister's side and begin blasting wolves.

Two pairs of witches were working together to douse the flames with blasts of frost magic. Another pair guarded them against the marauding wolves. A surprising number were about. She figured she'd seen upward of thirty, which was roughly the same number as the response force. One raced at her, and she stabbed out her left hand and covered it with lightning. It let out a shrill keen, then hit the ground and slid a couple of feet. Unconscious or dead, it was out of the fight for the moment.

She didn't have time to enjoy her success since Brianna shoved her out of the path of the wolf that flew between them. Her sister growled, "Where are they all coming from?"

Cait searched the area but didn't see a central source for their enemies. "They're everywhere. Not the smartest strategy."

Brianna laughed. "Let's show them the error of their ways. On me." Cait drew her shillelagh from her back and ran beside her sister. Their path took them to a trio of wolves that had just run down several Westport citizens. Brianna's shillelagh crushed the first one's skull before they knew they were under attack. Cait's blow caught another on the flank and staved in its ribs.

The wolf turned and leapt at her, fury overwhelming its good sense, and she nailed the same ribs with her backstroke. Her foe flew to the side, struck the ground, and began to crawl toward the tree line. Cait stepped forward and brought her shillelagh down on its head to end its attempt to escape.

As Brianna finished the other one, Cait said, "I wonder why it went toward the trees."

Her sister replied, "Uh, because they live in the woods?"

"Yeah, I suppose."

Brianna shoved her. "Quit using your brain and switch to your fists and magic. We have more wolves to kill."

---

Rebecca watched the pair of witches as they moved back into the battle—the one who had been staring at the tree line and the other who was clearly related to her. She'd ached to blast the women but had restrained herself by focusing on the larger picture. The portals bringing in defenders had stopped appearing, which meant that they'd drawn off whoever was going to be pulled into the town's defense.

She opened a portal back to the gathering area, raised her voice, and called, "The first phase is a success."

Luciana gave a cry of victory, echoed by the surrounding wolves. She ordered, "Second group, get to it."

Rebecca summoned a portal to the woods near the witches' village, and the main body of wolves charged through it.

---

Aisling wasn't a member of the first response force, which filled her with annoyance. Since she'd been instrumental in putting defenses around the coven, it made sense that she should be part of monitoring them, she supposed. She was looking through the eyes of her mechanical bird as it flew through the woods in a circle around the village. Its autopilot took care of weaving past trunks and through branches. The frequent adjustments, though effective, inspired a slight case of nausea in its rider.

A glow to the side caught her eye, and she took direct control of the bird to veer toward it. The illumination demarcated the boundaries of an open portal that flickered as wolves streamed out of it and dashed away to both sides. The shock of the sight disconnected her from the bird, and she gasped in alarm. Then she pulled her wits together and reached up to touch the earring that was magically connected to the one her sister wore.

She activated the channel and shouted, "Cait. They're about to attack the coven." Message delivered, she ran for the door to alert the reserve defense force that they were in imminent danger.

# CHAPTER SEVENTEEN

Cait snapped to Aza, *Where's Delsanra?*

*Other end of town.*

*Meet me there.* With a growl at the destruction around her, she ran at top speed until she found Delsanra. "An attack on the coven."

He cursed and shook his head. "I'm needed here. You go. I'll send others back after you."

She nodded, sent, *Aza, we're going,* and opened a portal. The dragon swooped down and through, and she followed him into the center of the clearing. People were running from the houses, although no wolves were yet in evidence. The reserve force was a mix of skilled fighters and people who generally didn't take part in combat. The latter were strong with magic, if not weapons, and were fully capable of defending the coven.

Cait found Aisling among them and asked, "What do you have?"

Her sister gestured with one of the swords she held.

"Portal's over that way, but the wolves were moving around the sides. They could come from anywhere."

She replied, "Or everywhere, more likely."

Sashura's magically amplified voice rang out. "Assemble in the center. Guard outward." They'd practiced this too, and Cait ran to find a place in line. She pulled out an energy potion and took a drink to replenish her power. She offered it to her sister, who shook her head. "I've got one, thanks."

Cait asked, "You okay?" Aisling radiated a fury that Cait had never seen in her.

"I'm tired of this. Tired of feeling threatened. I'm starting to think Brianna was right and we should have gone in, found the leaders, and dragged them off to prison."

Cait clarified, "Brianna wanted to kill them."

Aisling barked a laugh. "Well, I'm not *totally* like her. Heaven forbid that should ever happen."

Amusement vanished as wolves boiled out of the forest. Sashura yelled, "Shields," and barriers of all kinds except shadow snapped up around the circle. Much of their practice had been to learn how to properly overlap them to create a stronger defense. It wasn't an ancient phalanx formation, but it served the same purpose.

The wolves, unfortunately, were smarter than their animal counterparts. Instead of trying to overpower the defense, they jumped up and over the witches and dashed across to attack those facing in the opposite direction. Sashura yelled, "Pairs," the order to form teams with the witch beside them. Cait and Aisling spun to engage the wolves charging them.

A shout of terror and pain came from the side of the

clearing where Aisling had said the portal was located as a fireball slammed into a section of the defenders who had turned to face the wolves. Some had shields up at their backs in an abundance of caution, but others went down under the surprise assault. Cait reinforced the shields around her and swung her shillelagh like a baseball bat to knock the nearest wolf out of the fight, then raked lightning over a pair that was moving in her direction.

A shout from Aisling caused her to duck a leaping wolf. Her sister's twin swords sliced gouges in its flank, and it hit the ground hard and wailed in pain. Aisling flicked her fingers out, and a force bolt slammed it into unconsciousness or worse. Another wolf followed it, and Cait met that one with a burst of force magic, intending to knock it out of the air. Aza struck at the same moment, grabbed the wolf in his claws, and hurled it into the trees. She called, "Thanks, buddy."

He replied, *Don't mention it. Be careful.*

She countered, *Keep your wits about you. I know how tempting all these wolves must be.*

Laughter came across their connection. *You're not wrong. You know me well.*

She was drawn back into the battle as a witch beside her was tackled to the ground. Before the attacker could savage the woman's throat, Cait kicked out with all her strength and knocked the wolf a few feet away. It rushed at her with a snarl, and she swung her shillelagh to distract it. With her left hand, she drew Eclipse. The club forced it to go low to evade, and she dropped to one knee and plunged the dagger into its back where its spine met its neck, ending its participation in the fight.

Shouts of alarm came from all around her as another wave of wolves boiled out of the woods. She rose and snarled, "Where the hell are they coming from?" No one answered. Aisling was fighting off two wolves, pointing one sword toward each to keep them at bay. Cait's quick survey of the battlefield showed that the witches were holding their own at the moment but the wolves were grinding them down. Each loss the coven incurred was far more damaging than the loss of a wolf to the pack.

Cait slipped her shillelagh into its back harness and drew her pistol. Distance fire was too great a risk in this crowd, and she couldn't afford to miss. What she *could* do was run up directly beside the wolves and shoot them, so that was what she did. One after the next, she charged wolves who were occupied with other things and put bullets into them. She took down ten with her first magazine and sheathed Eclipse while she reloaded the weapon. Another seven fell before a wolf tackled her from behind and sent her pistol tumbling across the ground.

Aza swooped and plucked the wolf off her, then flew up and dropped it outside the main battle area. The wolf yowled on its way down, but the noise stopped in mid-scream when it hit the earth. Aisling was a dervish with her swords, making quick cuts to drive the wolves away from other people rather than focusing on scoring kills. Cait drew her shillelagh and dagger again as she ran. When she reached her sister, she asked, "Where are Mom and Dad?"

Aisling whipped her swords in an X to dissuade a wolf from attacking her. It made the wise choice to run off in search of a less dangerous opponent. She replied, "Guarding the non-combatants."

Since her mother was one of the strongest witches in the coven, it was logical that she would keep their elders and children safe from the attackers. One house was more thickly built than the rest, with strong locks on the doors and an underground cave to retreat to if necessary. Fortunately, so far, it didn't appear as if the wolves were interested in anyone other than the combatants in the center.

When the third wave of wolves rushed out of the forest, Cait groaned. Two peals of thunder rang out, the signal for a dire threat, and portals opened as the defenders in Westport surged back to defend the coven.

---

Rebecca watched the battle from the tree line. She'd thrown a couple of fireballs into the fray, but the witch who seemed to be in charge had looked directly at her after one of them, so she'd stopped and moved. Drawing attention was the worst thing she could do. Even if this fight turned out to be decisive, which she doubted, she couldn't risk being delayed.

She felt in her bones that the moment was right. Her destiny was at hand. She opened a portal and launched four fireballs in a high arc toward the center of the battle to add to the chaos, then stepped through and let it close behind her. Luciana was waiting. The wolves' leader asked, "How goes the battle?"

Rebecca smiled. "Very well. Your brothers and sisters might win the day at the coven. Now, let's go ensure we maintain power over this place for all time." She opened another rift to connect the staging area and the remaining wolves to the base of Croagh Patrick. She was unable to portal onto the mountain, which had surprised her when she'd discovered it. The guardian spirit apparently still held *some* power despite her efforts to diminish him by interfering with the connection to Stonehenge. *It matters not. Soon, I will control the mountain, and he will be no more.*

She charged through and shoved magic into her muscles to keep up with the wolves who rushed up the path leading to her, and their, final objective.

---

Cait stumbled and nearly fell but caught herself. She turned the momentary weakness into a tumbling roll out of the way of the wolf stalking her. Fear coursed through her veins, but she recognized it wasn't hers. The sensation had the feel of the spectral fox, and she put the pieces together.

She grabbed Aisling. "Be careful. I have to go."

Her sister didn't argue, just moved to locate a new witch to partner with. Cait sent, *Aza. I need to find Delsanra and Sashura.* The dragon guided her through the melee until she reached the pair, who were fighting near each other, ripping through wolves like a hurricane of steel and magic. She said, "I think this was all a feint. Croagh Patrick is under attack. If it falls, the land itself will become our enemy."

The coven's two prime warriors exchanged glances, then nodded. Delsanra said, "We can't afford to take anyone away from the defense of the coven."

Her spirits fell, only to rise when Sashura finished,

"Except us. Let's go." Cait was almost overcome by the power of their trust in her. She shoved emotion out of her mind, sent, *Aza, with me,* and opened a portal to the plateau of the mountain, where she knew the true battle between the wolves and the witches would culminate.

# CHAPTER EIGHTEEN

Cait's portal brought her, Aza, Delsanra, and Sashura to the pinnacle of Croagh Patrick. Cait immediately sensed the weakening the fox had mentioned. Something was acting against the place to reduce its vitality, she guessed by cutting off the flow of power or directly opposing it. No enemies were visible, which was a relief.

Aza launched into the air, and after several seconds, he sent, *West side. About halfway up. Probably twenty wolves. Wait, make that twenty-five or twenty-six.*

Cait echoed his words to Delsanra and Sashura. The two exchanged glances, then Delsanra growled, "I'll attack first. Sashura, move in behind me, far enough back that they won't see you immediately. Caitriona, you're the rearguard."

She countered, "I should be with you to coordinate with Aza."

Sashura growled, "Your dragon is a warrior. Set him free to fight."

"You're sure?"

Delsanra replied, "I am," and dashed down the hill, which brought the conversation to an end. Sashura followed.

Cait sent to Aza, *Weapons free, buddy. Sashura and Delsanra are on the way to fight. Go dissuade some wolves from coming up the hill.*

His mental voice was filled with excitement. *You'll warn me if something happens I can help with?*

*Promise.*

*Be careful.* Their connection receded to its baseline, and she sensed him diving toward the group ascending the mountain. Cait paced the periphery of the summit. When she'd assigned Brianna to rearguard at the tower, she'd known it would annoy her sister. Now that she was in the same position, she realized it was far more irritating than she'd guessed at the time.

Cait reached for her pistol to check the magazine and realized it was still on the grass of the battlefield in the village. *Damn it. Stupid.* She drew Eclipse and was comforted by the touch of the dagger's power as it flowed through her. At the sensation, she remembered her energy potion and sipped it to restore the magic she'd used.

She detected something, either with her mundane or magical senses, and turned to the south as a figure reached the summit. Power radiated from the woman, who was clad in a long dress or robes. Cait said, "You must be the mysterious person helping the wolves."

The other woman nodded. "I am. And you are, what, the coven's best warrior?" Her tone was confident, even condescending.

Cait shook her head. "No, they're down on the side of

the mountain dealing with the wolves, as you apparently expected them to be."

The new arrival gave a thin smile. "You are correct. I'd figured there was only a forty percent chance that they would leave someone behind since they knew where the attack was coming from."

Cait smiled. "Sorry to disappoint."

"Oh, it's no disappointment. I haven't gotten to kill anyone today so far. This will add the perfect bit of spice to taking possession of my mountain."

The spectral fox appeared to Cait's left and she turned toward it, careful not to let the other woman out of her sight. The new arrival also turned to the fox and shook her head with what was clearly mocking sadness. "How far you've fallen, Guardian. Never fear. Soon you will go to your endless rest." She gestured, spoke a word, and the fox vanished. Turning back to her, she said, "Now, where were we?"

Cait yanked her shillelagh from her back and snarled, "What have you done to him?"

The other woman rolled her eyes. "Banished him from the plateau. He's so weak now that he can't overcome me. Don't worry. Once I claim the mountain, I will eliminate him for real. He won't be in pain any longer."

"Over my dead body."

Her opponent smiled. "Exactly my thought."

---

Rebecca pushed magic into the armor she wore beneath her clothes. It had been specially designed to respond to her power and offered far greater protection than a standard defensive garment. The woman across from her seemed competent, but her hands were filled with weapons, which would work to Rebecca's advantage. She didn't use weapons often since her magic was almost always sufficient on its own.

She marshaled her power and snapped it out as she whipped both hands at her foe. The first dispatched a line of force aimed at the woman's feet. The second expelled a blast of force aimed at her head. That dual attack would put her in a bind since if she jumped to avoid the one, the other would catch her in the chest and hurl her off the mountaintop. When that happened, Rebecca could summon a shield to keep her off while she completed her conquest.

Her foe did neither of those things. She sliced her club down to intercept the line of force, which wrapped around it instead. The force blast struck the other woman's shields and dissipated, which caused Rebecca's eyes to widen in surprise. Despite claiming not to be the most powerful witch, her opponent's magical strength was formidable.

Rebecca yanked the weapon from her hand and hurled it over the side of the mountain, then ducked and slithered to the side as the other woman reached out with her magic and pulled the club back. Her evasion meant that the weapon sped past her head rather than through it. She circled, and her opponent mirrored her. "Well, you have some competence after all. That will make this far more satisfying."

Her foe smiled. "And here I thought you were going to

be some badass magical. You're just an average wacko with delusions of grandeur."

Rebecca laughed at the taunt. "Oh, I am *far* from average." She blasted electricity at the woman with her left hand and reached out with telekinesis for a large boulder at the edge of the plateau with the other. Her opponent's shield began to sparkle, and her electricity failed to penetrate it. As the rock came in from the side, her rival lifted her dagger and cast magic through it, causing the stone to shatter and fly in all directions.

Shrapnel peppered Rebecca's shield and fell to the dirt and grass at her feet. She laughed. "My, my, my. This will definitely be more fun than I thought." She gathered her power for the next attack.

Cait continued her slow circle with her eyes locked on the other woman. She had a sense of the battle below, channeled through Aza's feelings, and didn't want to pull the dragon away from the fight yet. The balance was still too even. The woman across from her was clearly a threat, but Cait thought she could manage her, especially since this was her home territory. Although her foe had weakened Croagh Patrick, the power wasn't gone.

A blast of fire came from one of the woman's hands. Cait dropped and rolled to the right, even though that was closer to the fire, to pass under the stream and avoid stumbling into whatever other attack she'd make. The woman moved to follow her, and Cait snapped the word to activate the warding circle she'd just dropped into. The magical barrier went up to block her enemy's power.

Cait wished she could go back in time and remember to retrieve her pistol since that would end the fight in an instant. Her opponent's dress would do nothing to defend the woman from an anti-cure-all. Instead, she pointed her weapons at the other woman, spoke the words to drop the ward, and slammed a cone of frost magic into the other woman's fire attack. The magics met in an explosion of water and steam.

Cait used the distraction to conceal her actions and hurled her shillelagh ahead at ankle level. Her foe snarled a curse and fell to the ground, to judge by the sounds. The stream of fire continued at an angle that confirmed it. That the other magical kept the attack going signaled her competence. Cait wasn't sure she could have done the same.

She circled, and the cone followed her. She turned her stream to frost and electricity, and the other woman cursed again. The magic dropped, and Cait's phased attack hit her foe's shields and outlined her in an oval of power as she stood up. Her opponent's expression was thunderous, and Cait idly wondered when she'd last been in a fair fight. She sent to Aza, *Break away when you can. I don't think I'm in imminent danger, but this woman's good.*

Aza replied, *Very soon. Two more, and I'm on my way.*

Cait grinned at the enthusiasm in the dragon's tone. Fair fights were overrated.

Rebecca had switched from amused to angry when the club had hit her. Now, she clamped down her will on the pain so she wouldn't limp and reveal that the blow had damaged her. The witch had accessed the power of the mountain, which she would've said was impossible, given all of her efforts to weaken it. That was fine. Two could play that game, and her foe had just outlived her usefulness as entertainment.

She opened herself to the flow of magic in the mountain. It resisted her at first, as it would until she had conquered it, but she was able to create a narrow channel to access the line of power beneath the rock. As her magic touched it, she felt the resonance of Stonehenge. She gathered that power to her and blasted the other woman with a double dose of lightning.

Her opponent snapped up a lightning shield that appeared to have fire flickering around the edges. The barrage of power was intense enough to drive her back toward the edge of the plateau. Rebecca advanced and maintained the assault, one hand aimed at the woman's head, the other at her chest. All she needed was for her foe to falter, just once. To trip, to take a step over the edge, to do anything that would break her concentration even for a moment. When that happened, Rebecca's power would rend the witch into pieces for the wolves to eat when they arrived.

Her foe seemed to realize the danger as she neared the edge of the plateau. Her retreat stopped, and for a moment, a balance held. Then the woman began to push back. Rebecca laughed. The other woman's magic was no match for the power line she channeled. The attempt would tire her, while with the flow of power coming to her, Rebecca would never tire.

She reveled in the feeling and the certainty that soon she would be victorious over the witch, the coven, and all the lands between Stonehenge and Croagh Patrick. Rebecca laughed.

Her connection with the mountain gave her just enough warning to snap up her shields as the dragon slammed into her out of nowhere.

Cait straightened, every pore in her body still sending pain signals to her brain from the enemy's sustained attack. She'd felt Aza coming and held her ground, but she had almost broken before the dragon's arrival. She expected to see that he'd knocked the woman unconscious and thought it was quite likely he'd killed her, given the speed she'd felt him build as he flew toward the battle.

The sight that greeted her was the opposite of what she'd anticipated. Aza was on the ground, trying and failing to regain his feet, clearly stunned. Her enemy was upright, covered in layers of shields. Cait couldn't imagine how much power and magic it had taken to negate his blow. She couldn't have done it. She whispered, "How?"

Like a rustle on the wind, the spectral fox's words caressed her ears. "Use the power of the mountain." She reached for him but found something else. Like a veil had been peeled away, she could feel the lines of magic that spread through the mountain like capillaries in a leaf, all funneling back to a single point. She sensed a branch and realized it headed to the east, which explained many things the fox had said.

Cait opened herself to it as the other woman launched another blast of power. The magic surged through her, and she crafted it into shields that broke the other woman's attack. She smiled when the power banished her pain. "I see why you wanted the mountain."

Her foe's face turned ugly. "Die, witch." The blast of lightning was the strongest she'd ever faced, and before today, it would have overwhelmed her shields and ended her. Cait knew that, and yet it was only as impactful as a wave reaching the point on the beach where it started to recede.

She called, "Surrender, and we can talk."

The other woman shouted, "Never!" Cait sensed her building power. What she planned to do with it was unknown, but it couldn't be good for Cait or anyone she loved. She reached out with the strength of the mountain and hit her opponent with a burst of force magic. It blasted her into one of the boulders along the periphery. The stone tumbled down the side, but not before the impact had broken the other woman's body.

Cait maintained her shields, walked over to her foe, and watched the disbelief harden on her face as life fled. She felt regret tempered with satisfaction at the elimination of the threat. The spectral fox flickered into view, and Cait took the mountain's power and channeled it into him. He grew almost solid, and his connection to the mountain, his unity with the power, was re-established.

She released the flow little by little, desperate to retain the pleasure that suffused her but knowing it was not hers to hold. When it was gone, she felt as awake and alert as she had ever been and was filled with the joy the magic had left behind.

The fox sat primly and gazed at her with a smile. "You've done it. The wolves are fleeing. The mountain is safe."

Aza bounded over. *We did it.*

Cait laughed and patted him on the shoulder. "We did. Fox, it's good to have you back. We need to talk later about how to make sure this never happens again. For now, though, Aza and I have to go help our people."

## CHAPTER NINETEEN

No one in Cait's family slept that night. She helped Delsanra and Sashura and several others search the woods for any remaining wolves. The others were exhausted but happy at the end because they found none. Cait felt like she might never need sleep again with the residual power from the mountain throbbing in her veins.

Aisling, who looked done in, remarked upon it in annoyance when Cait returned. She opened her mouth to explain but realized it would be impossible to convey the feeling. She settled for making a joke of it and helped the others cope by brewing strong pots of coffee and tea. Most of the kitchen was devoted to her mother's alchemy as she crafted healing potions. The process was time-intensive, even with the half-dozen talented volunteers she had working with her.

Cait spent hours running supplies from place to place since she wasn't skilled in healing beyond first aid. She bandaged some wounds and conjured snow for people to use in ice packs but otherwise stayed on the periphery of the healing effort. The coven's emergency plans detailed certain houses for certain things, like hers for creating healing potions, and Cait went to the one charged with feeding everyone.

Pots bubbled on every burner, filled with stew and porridge. Cait grabbed ingredients and mixed dough for bread, throwing little bits at Aza, who sat on the floor beside her. He snapped them out of the air and swallowed them but only stayed for a short time before he headed out for another flyover of the nearby woods. She was convinced the threat was ended, but the others didn't share her certainty.

Of course, none of them had felt what she'd felt on the mountain. Even now, she sensed the fox watching over the land.

After several hours, the coven was organized and taking care of itself. Cait walked through the grassy area where the battle had happened. The blood was still present, although the bodies of fallen witches and wolves had been removed. As she looked around, she could almost see the sparkle of the mountain's power on each blade of grass and tree in the forest. The feeling inside her, of connection to the land, to this place, was one she'd never acknowledged or understood before. She realized now, though, that it had to have been there all along, underpinning the prosperity of the coven for generations. *Whoever chose this spot to settle was very wise. It is definitely worth fighting for.*

Cait spotted her pistol, picked it up, and shoved it into the holster. It would be useless until she cleaned it. Sashura appeared on one side of the clearing at the head of a group of witches. She snapped, "Caitriona, with us." The other woman opened a portal that showed Westport on the opposite side. Cait told Aza to join her and walked through the moment he flew by.

The village was a mess. While the fires had all been extinguished, the bodies of wolves, citizens, and defenders were still visible on the streets. In places, the attackers had been separated from those they had killed, which Cait considered an appropriate gesture of respect for the fallen humans and witches. Sashura detailed a group of people to deal with that and ordered, "The rest of us, into the town hall."

An impromptu hospital had been set up in the building, and the healers immediately went to work. While magics like healing potions couldn't help non-magicals, simple applications of elemental power, such as the use of precision force magic to straighten broken bones, were well-known among the healers. Cait performed first aid where she could, although most of the people in the room had already been treated by Westport's medical personnel.

She didn't spot any severe cases and remarked on it to another of the witches. A doctor from Westport overheard. "Your people portaled the worst ones to the city, so they could get better care."

Cait rose. "How many did you lose?"

The man sighed. Another doctor, one Cait recognized from prior visits as both his business and personal life partner, stepped up beside him. The woman said, "The wolves appeared to be more interested in wounding people than killing them, at least at first. We've got a dozen dead, but it could've been much worse."

Cait nodded. That was good news. "How can I help?"

The first doctor shrugged. "Go make sure there's no one we've missed."

With Aza's help, Cait leaned into the connection between them and searched for signs of life as they walked and flew through the town. She found no one hiding and no wounded who hadn't gotten help, which was reassuring to everyone involved when she reported back. With nothing else demanding her attention, she helped clear the bodies from the street.

Night stretched into day and then into late afternoon by the time the family gathered again. Potions were still cooking in their kitchen, but others had brought food from the communal house, and they were glad to have it. Cait looked around the table at those she loved. Everyone was exhausted, and even she was starting to feel the effects of the long day, although she wasn't anywhere close to needing a bed.

Before they ate, her mother said, "Remember this day. It will become one of the tales told in the coven to the generations that succeed us. This moment where we rose to the occasion to preserve our way of life and protect our neighbors."

Everyone nodded, and her father broke the seriousness by saying, "If I don't eat this food, I'm going to fall asleep in it." They all laughed and attacked the meal with gusto. Cait slipped Aza a piece of bread under the table, but the way the dragon took it told her he was tired, too.

She asked, "How many did we lose?"

Brianna growled, "About a fourth of our fighting force."

Her mother added, "As well as some non-fighters who

were in the wrong place at the wrong time when the wolves attacked."

Cait sighed. "It was worth it, you know. Can you feel it?"

Aisling asked, "What?"

"A sense of rightness, or maybe of power. The guardian spirit on the mountain is strong again, and his protection spreads over us."

Her younger sister replied, "I thought I saw him a couple of times while I was watching the mountain, as you asked us to do. He didn't talk to me."

Cait nodded. "He was weakened by something the woman I fought did to him, but now he's back to full strength, although he says there's still a problem in the east." Seeing their expressions tighten, she clarified, "Far from here, to the east."

Brianna asked, "Do you know what it is?"

"No, and I don't have the bandwidth to figure it out right now, but the coven should keep it in mind." Her lips turned down as a thought occurred to her. "With all those losses, will the coven still be viable?" They had never possessed excess numbers, and losing so many people would be a blow.

Her mother smiled. "As long as we find strong partners from outside the coven to have children with, Caitriona, we'll be fine."

Everyone laughed, and Cait blushed. Brianna pointed that out, which led to more laughter at Cait's expense. She buried her face in her hands and shook her head. "You guys suck."

Aza sent, *It's good to hear them laughing.*

She replied, *One hundred percent agree, buddy. Whatever darkness was encroaching on our lives, it's lifted now, and I think I established a connection with the mountain. We will have to come back more often so I can help the fox protect this place.*

He snorted. *You're just making an excuse to see Will.*

Cait grinned inwardly, still being barraged by mocking comments from her family. *I'm not going to lie. That will be a bonus.*

# CHAPTER TWENTY

Victor Huff gazed around the dining room he'd reserved in Boston's most exclusive private club. He had deployed his people to the place earlier to watch over the chefs and the restaurant's staff. The meeting was important, and he didn't want anything stupid like an assassination attempt to interrupt it. He had no reason to think any particular danger threatened at the moment but knew he would always be a target for someone.

If he had his way, he would become a target for a large number of people in the very near future.

He had dressed in a bespoke business suit, an imported silk tie, an expensive shirt, and his best pair of shoes. The cufflinks at his wrists had belonged to his father and were only worn on special occasions. His watch was one of the most prized pieces in his collection, a Patek Phillipe he'd purchased at an auction. He thought of his clothes as armor because they showed the enemy that he was ready for battle.

His executive assistant, girlfriend, and true partner

Eliza stood beside him in a brilliant red dress and matching pumps. Her long nails were painted to match the outfit. He doubted she was wearing the poison tips today but wasn't positive. He'd made it a practice to avoid startling her, ever. Victor was confident she would never turn on him, but if she did, he'd be dead before he realized it had happened.

You had to trust somebody. No one could do everything alone.

That was the point of tonight's meeting. He had spent several years working up to this moment, making the contacts he needed and donating money to almost every legitimate political campaign. He hadn't created Perpetuity, but when he became aware of its existence, he had harnessed it to his will.

It formed the backbone of his plans. It provided contacts at the top of the monetary food chain, connected him to the most powerful political candidates and influencers, and granted him control of a grassroots army ready to launch a campaign on behalf of him or any candidate he supported.

The men coming to visit today knew all that. What they didn't know was that he'd also used the organization to discover talent of a different kind. Those people had been siphoned away from the main group to create a team loyal to him personally. They were a backup plan to a backup plan, and if things went right tonight, they would probably never be needed.

The room was elegant and comfortable. All four walls were painted a soft yellow, and dark wood accents filled the place. The table was covered with a brilliant blue tablecloth, and the plates upon it were bright white with gold designs around the edges. Heavy utensils matched the edging, as did the candelabras. Their beeswax candles spread a pleasant scent through the room. It was as perfect as it could be for his moment of triumph.

The far door opened, and the first of his guests arrived. He whispered, "Here we go."

Eliza whispered back, "You'll be amazing."

He laughed softly. "How about you dazzle them all so I don't have to be?" She didn't reply but stayed at his side while he greeted each person who entered the room as if they were the most important being on the planet. When the other ten were assembled, he claimed the seat at one end of the table, and she took the one on the opposite end.

The dinner service began, and they spent the time in conversation about events in the city, the larger political picture, and other things he couldn't care less about at the moment. He, as usual, was focused on the end game. These preliminary discussions didn't interest him. Nonetheless, he allowed himself to enjoy the parts of the meal he could, namely the sight of his beautiful partner at the other end of the table and the amazing cuisine provided by the restaurant.

The seven-course meal included fresh lobster with filet mignon as its centerpiece, and dessert was his choice, apple pie with cinnamon ice cream, arguably the most American thing ever. When everyone had finished eating and the dishes had been taken away, spirits and coffee were served, and the tuxedoed chief server circled the table with a humidor filled with top-end cigars.

When everyone was properly satisfied and the staff

banished from the room, Victor began, "So. We've had a fine meal, and now it's time for business. Give me the good news."

A man on the right side of the table cleared his throat and waved his cigar. "It might not be as good as you hoped, Victor."

He kept his face still and his voice neutral with an effort. "Why is that?"

Another replied, "You're not well-known enough. The public will not accept you as the choice. They don't know you."

He watched who looked at who and realized the group had discussed this ahead of time. *Smart on their part.* "After all the money I've given you? After the candidates I've donated to? After the network I've helped build, this is the answer?"

One of the men nearest him made a calming gesture as if he were patting a dog. "We're not saying it's impossible, Victor, only that it can't be right now. We need to raise your profile, that's all. This time next year, we'll be able to make it happen."

Victor forced himself not to react. The response had taken him by surprise. It went against what they'd all been telling him so far, and the suspicious part of his mind wondered if they'd been playing him all along. He searched each face, not speaking, and decided they hadn't been dishonest. Maybe misinformed, or perhaps they'd overestimated their sway with the essential people. He said, "Raise my profile. I presume you have suggestions for how to accomplish that."

Many of them did, which they shared at length. Their

relief at his reaction was evident in the way they talked, in their expressions, and in the fact that none of them had tried to flee the restaurant. Victor partitioned a portion of his mind to remember the things they were saying for later reference and looked down at the table. Eliza tapped a fingernail on its surface while looking him in the eye.

He gave a slight shake of his head. Had it been betrayal rather than incompetence, he might've chosen otherwise and painted the walls of the room red with the blood of these idiots, but no. They might still prove useful. He allowed the discussion to continue for a half-hour longer, then brought the meeting to a close. It wasn't the most polite dismissal, but neither was it as sharp as he would have preferred.

After the last guest exited, a man who looked very much like him and was dressed in an identical suit stepped into the room. Victor smiled at his body double. "Good meal?"

The other man's voice even sounded like his. "Chef's table, boss. From the look on your face, I had a better experience than you did."

"Well, you deserve it for putting yourself in the crosshairs for me time and again. Head on down to the car." After he departed, another of Victor's assistants opened a portal to the corner of the apartment that would permit magic. They stepped through, then went into the living room.

He loosened his tie and undid the top button on his shirt, then fell onto a couch. "Damn political people. More visible, they say. What have they been doing for the last year?"

Eliza placed a tumbler of whiskey in his hand and sat on the edge of the couch, twisting to put her legs over his lap. "They're not as competent as one would like, but they're the only game in town, right?"

He took a sip and paused to appreciate the flavor of the whiskey. "I'm not willing to wait a year."

She shrugged. "Tell me who you want killed, and I'll make it happen."

He patted her legs. "I know you would. But no, I need you with me. I have a different idea. It means changing some of our plans. I'd intended to move subtly in a variety of areas, but if they want visibility, I'll give them a show no one will forget."

Eliza replied, "Are you sure?"

"We've been building the capacity. It's just a matter of deploying it differently. Put out the call. Get everyone into town and gather them together."

She rose and looked down at him. "I do so love it when you're decisive."

He laughed. "Well then, you're going to adore the next few days."

# CHAPTER TWENTY-ONE

Cait knocked on Sabrina's door with her head since both arms were filled with plastic bags. Her friend opened it, grabbed a portion of her burden, and carried the goodies over to the dining room table while Cait followed. They sorted out the small cardboard boxes. Every few weeks, on a Monday night, they met to eat way too much food from a Chinese restaurant, and this was that evening.

After the first time, she'd asked Yoshino for a restaurant recommendation, and since then, the quality had increased with each new place they tried. Sabrina had set out a pot of tea and plates, and they loaded them with egg rolls, dim sum, fried dumplings, and Crab Rangoon. They munched happily and conversed between bites. Sabrina said, "Simon's party went well, I thought."

Cait nodded and used her chopsticks to send a steamed dumpling in an arc toward where Aza lay nearby. The dragon caught it with ease. *More.*

She laughed, shared his comment with Sabrina, and unfolded one of the containers on the floor so he could serve himself. It was always amusing that when eating Chinese food, the dragon was almost dainty, downing it piece by piece rather than devouring it like he did the fish that was his primary sustenance. Cait replied, "Totally agree. A great time was had by all, and I think he was grateful for the sendoff."

"Not as grateful as he is to be retired, though."

Cait chuckled. "That goes without saying. You were right. His post-marshal life looks good on him."

Sabrina gestured vaguely with her chopsticks. "I have to say, I didn't think it would work out at first, but Susan is a good fit."

"Agreed. I had reservations in those early days, too. She comes off as super tough, but there's a sharp mind behind the bluster."

The infomancer grinned. "An area in which you are lacking."

Cait mock shivered. "So cold, so rude."

Sabrina laughed. "You all are a good team, I think. Fortunately, Clement and Garrett are fairly laid back. I've worked with marshals who were annoyingly gung ho."

She snorted. "Yeah, me too. And hyper-competitive, which didn't make my status as a magical any more acceptable to them."

"I can see where that might be the case."

Cait scooped orange chicken onto her plate, along with a dollop of fried rice. "I fit in well here, I think."

Sabrina paused with her chopsticks halfway to her mouth. "You say that like it's temporary."

Cait sighed. "I don't think it is, and I hope it's not, but things back home have become complicated."

Sabrina's brow knitted in concern. "The wolves?"

"No. Well, kind of. It's like this." Cait described the battle against the wolves and the reclaiming of the mountain. "And now we have to work together in a time of healing and rebuilding. That, as my mother has pointed out, involves children, especially those of strong witches."

Sabrina laughed. "Trust her to take advantage of the situation."

"They must teach you that during childbirth classes."

"That would explain a lot."

She flicked a piece of chicken toward Aza, and he snapped it out of the air. "Anyway, Will and I are getting along pretty well and have agreed to spend more time together. I don't know if that will take me away from Boston more often or if he'll join me here or what, but it's two more obligations that have moved to the top of my personal pile."

Sabrina ate the bite she'd been holding in midair, chewed, and swallowed. "It's like anything, I suppose. Enjoy what you can when you can, whether it's work or play." She snagged a piece of chicken with her chopsticks and flicked it at Aza. "Or Chinese food."

After the meal, they headed to the living room with a bottle of wine, a ritual that had become a Boston-life touchstone for Cait. She'd had friends outside the coven before, but none so deep as Sabrina. It was the thing she thought about with the most regret when she considered leaving Boston behind, even more than leaving the marshals.

However, Will was right. Portals made distance evaporate. Basing her life in Ireland didn't mean letting go of everything she'd built here.

Sabrina brought her out of her reverie with an offhand comment. "Oh, I decoded more stuff from the Cui Siwang hack."

Cait sighed and shook her head. "You do that on purpose."

Sabrina replied innocently, "What?"

"Wait until a calm moment to drop an information bomb just to rattle my brain."

The other woman laughed. "An apt description. Yeah, I do. Fortunately, your brain has minimal defenses."

Cait scowled at her friend. "You're going to make me ask, aren't you?"

"Yep."

*Then again, maybe getting some distance from Sabrina would make the heart grow fonder.* Through dramatically gritted teeth, she forced out the words, "What. Did you. Discover?"

"The son, Shao, was scheduled to fly in today."

She groaned at the memory of their last go-round. "I don't think I can be Lexi at the bar again. Too embarrassing."

Sabrina laughed. "Aw, come on. I want to hear you do the drunken strumpet thing again."

"Strumpet?"

"So I like classic English romance novels. What?" They shared a laugh, then Sabrina suggested, "Rooftop watch?"

Cait closed her eyes in anticipated pain. "So boring. How about a drone?"

The infomancer shrugged. "Watching with a drone is

easy. Following, less so. I thought you wanted to track him this time?"

"That's true. Aza, why don't you make yourself useful? You can follow him while I sleep."

The dragon, who was lying on the floor with his chin on his paws, didn't open his eyes. *Do you really want that?*

Cait thought about it, then sighed heavily. "No, I don't want you out there on your own unsupervised." His mouth stretched in a grin.

She examined her wine glass, which still had a couple of swallows remaining, then emptied it. She pushed up off the couch and headed for the kitchen. "I hope you have some strong coffee to counteract that wine and maybe a thermos to take with me."

Her host rose to assist. "We'll find something. Don't worry; it won't be *too* boring. I can read to you from my latest novel while you watch."

Cait let her head fall forward to thump one of the cabinets. "Heaven save me from my friends."

Sabrina laughed, and Aza echoed it in her mind. The infomancer said, "No one's coming to rescue you. You're stuck with us."

# CHAPTER TWENTY-TWO

Carl locked the outer door of his shielded ready room, then twisted and pulled the knob to make sure it was closed. He'd spent a restless day feeling that his pursuit of revenge against Huff wasn't moving quickly enough and had summoned his lieutenants back to the warehouse to talk things over.

He walked through the open portion of the building first, exchanging words or handshakes with the people who were taking advantage of the new digs. This was their safe place when they left their work on the streets. Here, they could release the constant tension of the city's current situation. Each was skilled in counter surveillance and reached the refuge by indirect routes, so no enemy could track them to the location.

That was only the first level of protection. Hidden watchers were positioned in all directions, and an info-mancer team located in the suburbs controlled cameras and drones that kept a wary eye on the Thorns' territory. It wasn't an impregnable fortress by any means, but it was the best he could do to meet his and his people's safety needs while still maintaining some sense of normalcy for the Thorns.

The people in the building tonight were doing better than they had been in the days before. Their moods had improved and their confidence had increased when word of the leaders' previous meeting had deliberately been leaked to them. It gave them the impression that things were moving and that those in charge were thinking, which was enough for most of them.

To him, it seemed like they'd achieved forward momentum for the first time in forever. He stepped into the sectioned-off area that was their meeting space and began, "Good feelings in here tonight. Let's have the reports."

The man who oversaw the money replied, "We made the initial move on the office space. We should have a contract and be ready to close by midweek."

Carl raised an eyebrow. "So fast?"

His infomancer, who was part of the office-securing mission, sniffed. "The building has a ton of empty offices. We've agreed to pay a premium for quick entry and explained that we're a game design company that needs big bandwidth fast. They're almost tripping over themselves to get us in there."

"The company will pass inspection?"

The man nodded. "Absolutely. It *is* a small game design company. The project is a real one, and we've had little involvement with it thus far. We bankrolled it and set it free. Only the person in charge knows about the connection to the Thorns."

"Perfect. Well done." Both men smiled at the compliment. "And the others?"

His intelligence specialist said, "We've chosen the woman for the honeypot." She slid a large envelope down the table to him, and he opened it to find a photo of a brunette in her twenties who was an absolute stunner.

"Wow. Good choice, but she looks young. Does she have what it takes?"

His subordinate smiled. "She's been a street soldier for years. She'll do fine."

*Things are getting better and better.* "How soon can we put her in play?"

"She needs a little polish and some practice at being fancy, so she'll fit in around Huff. Two weeks."

Carl shook his head. "Make it one." She nodded. It was good to have competent people. "Okay then, let's talk about infiltrating Huff's staff—"

The warehouse erupted in a cacophony that made it seem like an explosion had gone off over their heads. Glass flew from the upper windows and descended on them in a shower as black-clad figures slid down ropes that dropped into the building.

The fact that their meeting space had four walls but no ceiling had never been more noticeable than at that moment. Carl's hands moved automatically to pull up his shirt and yank out one pistol, then repeat the process with the other as he ran out of the room to the main area.

The intruders wore body armor with full motorcycle-style helmets that eliminated any chance of identifying them. He presumed they would also be highly protective, so he lowered his aim and shot at legs and feet as the new arrivals hit the floor. His people had reacted to the invasion in different ways. Some ran directly at the invaders and attempted to tackle them. Others rushed toward weapons that hadn't been at hand. Only a few had been armed at the moment of the break-in, and he was the only one to get off a shot before their enemies fired.

Their suppressed rifles belched bullets with a series of soft pops rather than the harsh bark of his pistols, but the aftermath was loud enough to make up for it. Screams from his people filled the space as they went down, interspersed with shouted commands to each other to counterattack. The soldier closest to Carl turned to face him.

He reflexively reached for his magic to shield, then the meaning of the itch at the back of his head that had started a moment before the assault began penetrated his brain. An anti-magic field had been dropped on the warehouse. He didn't know the how of it, but he realized in an instant that these people were the ones who had killed Cynthia.

Carl snarled, "Huff," under his breath, rushed to meet the one coming for him, and dodged to the side as the figure tried to shoot him. The evasion delivered him to cover behind a set of old file cabinets they'd found during the move-in and repurposed to hold body armor and other gear. Bullets banged off the metal and ricocheted to spark on the floor. Carl used the cover to dart along the wall of the planning room to the back of the warehouse. From there, he skirted the side of the building in a crouch behind pallets that had been moved out of the main area and looked for an opportunity to thin the enemy's numbers.

One of his soldiers ran past him, hit the door in the outer wall, and passed through it to freedom. The respite was only momentary, however, since he immediately staggered back through the door, his torso riddled with bloody bullet holes. Carl shouted, "They've got the place surrounded. Fight, damn you."

The pallet he was hiding behind took fire. He ran along the edge of the building, back the way he had come and away from the man who'd tried to escape. The corner provided momentary security, and he pulled out his phone. A sequence of presses sent out an alert to his people to get off the streets and find safety. At first, he'd believed they might fight off this attack, but it was now a toss-up at best. However, if this was an all-out assault on the Thorns, a large portion of the gang might get away.

He shoved the phone into his pocket and crept along the back wall. The battle was in full bloom, and the people he'd been meeting with a few moments before had thrown themselves into the thick of it like the good leaders they were. Two were down, and another bullet took out his demolitions expert. The explosion that followed caught several enemies in its blast radius.

Carl chuckled at the appropriateness that his subordinate—and friend, he admitted—had rigged a dead man switch before he ran into battle. He sighted on the back of the nearest large helmet and pulled his triggers six times in rapid succession. The barrage got through and the figure fell, but Carl was driven back into cover by more enemy gunfire.

The red hair of his intelligence specialist caught his eye as she ran toward him, but three streams of bullets converged on her before she could reach safety. She fell, and her lifeless eyes stared at him. He shook his head as if she'd accused him of betraying her. *I'm sorry.*

The sight broke something in him. He wasn't able to defeat these enemies. He didn't have the people to do it, plus he'd sent any available reinforcements off to their own hiding places with his earlier alarm. That had been the right thing to do, but the choice had cost him any possibility of winning this battle.

He jolted to his feet and ran toward his receiving room in the corner of the building. A single black-suited guard stood in the way, facing the main room. Carl emptied his pistols into the figure, and his bullets marched up the figure's side from shin to shoulder. His enemy went down, and Carl hurdled the body, unlocked the door, and closed himself in his outer receiving room. He quickly secured the locks, then paused to catch his breath.

The room was specially crafted to insulate against exterior signals, which meant he couldn't use his phone from inside. It also meant the anti-magic field wasn't able to penetrate. He snapped up his shields and reloaded his pistols with the idea of going out to see if anyone else could be rescued.

The delay allowed rationality to creep into his brain. Carl sighed heavily at the realization that returning would only get him killed. This battle was lost. The building didn't matter, only the people in it, and he could do nothing for them. They were already down or would be before he could make a difference.

He shoved the pistols into his belt, used magic to unlock his receiving chamber, stepped in, and closed the door behind him. Doing so eliminated the risk of anyone who might break into the outer room seeing his bunker before he escaped. Plus, this space was double-protected from the anti-magic emitters. He opened the portal and stepped through to safety.

It closed behind him, and Carl sank to the floor on his knees, then leaned forward until his head touched the ground. He'd taken so many hits lately that it was hard to maintain the strength to go on. First Cynthia, then his people. He straightened with an inward snarl and screamed his rage at the ceiling to expel the emotion, as he'd been taught to do during his Syndicate training.

When he'd yelled himself hoarse, he took all the remaining fury, anger, and disappointment within, bundled them up, and threw them into a figurative fire. Cold calculation replaced every other feeling as he watched them burn in his mind's eye. *My life in Boston is done. It's time for me to head back and rejoin the Syndicate.* His lips twisted in a cruel smile. *After I kill Victor-freaking-Huff.*

# CHAPTER TWENTY-THREE

Yoshino passed through the outer guards at the top of the staircase and entered the second floor of the restaurant behind Kono. Her lieutenants were already assembled, each kneeling on cushions positioned around the low dining table. Kono escorted her to the head and offered his hand for support as she gracefully flowed to her knees. As always, she appreciated the gesture but didn't require the assistance. He arranged her simple white robes and adjusted her hair, which was held in place by her ivory chopstick-style hairpins.

He moved to his end of the table, and she nodded at the guard. He spoke a few words, and servers bearing appetizers entered. As the plates were set among them, the Dragons' leaders exchanged small talk. The conversation flowed easily, as it always did, but today she detected an edge of tension in most of them. It wasn't an uncommon occurrence, and given the current situation, it was understandable.

Two, however, appeared especially jumpy. Xie, the

leader of her infomancers and technology specialist, seemed to vibrate with discomfort. Yoshino had seen it in her before and had diagnosed its cause as a feeling of inferiority compared to her hierarchical peers. She did her best to build the younger woman up on every occasion possible, but it was true that the age difference between her and the others around the table was substantial.

In addition to life experience, they also had more concrete evidence of success to offer than the infomancer did. Those things in combination could make one doubt oneself. For her part, Yoshino harbored no reservations about her subordinate and still saw the other woman as the best pick for second-in-command to Kono if something happened to her.

That Quan also seemed antsy was not as easily explained. Perhaps his report would show that his area had been less successful than the others', which would be a concern worthy of attention. At each meeting, someone was the most successful and someone the least. While she did not make judgments on such a transitory basis, the loss of face caused by being in the trailing position was bound to be damaging to one's ego. And ego, experience had proven again and again, was what drove people at the top level of any organization.

A sudden surge of noise from below caused everyone in the room to leap to their feet. Kono snapped his fingers, and the guard by the door ran out. He pulled his pistol and stood near the doorway. Quan shouted, "Konya, Inzani, with me." The trio ran for the exit, and Kono moved out of the way to let them pass.

Yoshino headed to the side of the room. Kono's most

trusted guard was always on the security team that cleared locations for her use and, as part of the preparation, hid a sword for her and an additional pistol for Kono. The practice was known only to the three of them. She'd automatically identified the marked panel when she came in and opened it now to retrieve the items.

She handed the gun to Xie, who accepted it with a trembling hand. Yoshino spoke as if to a nervous child. "Calm yourself. Likely it is nothing. You will stand over there in the far corner with me." She moved to that position and called, "Kono. Lock the door and join us." He turned to stare a question at her, then nodded in agreement. When he arrived, she attempted a shield. A sense of dread settled inside her when the magic failed to come to her call. "They have anti-magic emitters. Send out the emergency alert."

Kono reached for his phone and busied himself for a moment. "Sent."

"Good. Now, move to my right." Yoshino held the scabbard in her left hand and the sword hilt in her right. Her allies stood on either side of her with their pistols pointed at the door. "Now we wait."

---

Cait crouched on the rooftop across from Shao's penthouse, staring at the windows with the magnification provided by the faceplate of her infiltration suit. She started when her phone buzzed in an unfamiliar pattern. She looked down and saw a message from Kono that had apparently been broadcast to everyone in the Dragons, which now included her, given the honorary status Yoshino had bestowed upon her. It signaled a high alert and gave a street address. Cait called it up and recognized it as a restaurant where she'd met with Yoshino. She snapped, "Something's going down with the Dragons."

Sabrina replied, "I'll send a drone over there."

"Keep an eye on our friend. I'm going, too." *Aza, with me.*

It took the dragon a few seconds to get there, and she had the portal open when he arrived. They moved through, and she dashed across the street toward the restaurant while he soared into the sky. She hoped no one had seen them together but didn't have the free mental cycles to worry about it. The street-level windows had all been blown in, and the sounds of gunfire spilled out from inside. Cait recognized the black-clad figures and growled, "Dammit, it's the Cui Siwang again. Those bastards won't quit."

Aza reported, *People in black moving on the rooftop nearby.*

Cait cursed and replied, *If you can pick off stragglers without revealing yourself, go for it. Otherwise, don't risk being seen.* She jumped through the window, put her pistol against the back of one of the soldiers, and pulled the trigger three times. He went down when the close-up shots defeated his armor's protection.

She snapped up a shield but it didn't come, which generated another curse from her. She threw herself to the side to get behind a table that had been flipped over. Gunfire slammed into it, and she grabbed a taser grenade from her belt. She hurled it, then sent a second in a different direction. Both went off, and she popped up out of cover.

One of Yoshino's people was pointing a weapon at her, and she dipped a hand into her belt and pulled out the token the Dragons' leader had given her. The man immediately dropped his barrel, sketched a bow, and went back to shooting at the enemy soldiers. Her arrival had caused a lull in the battle while its participants adjusted to the changed situation, though by her estimation, the other side still had a numerical advantage.

She spotted two people in suits on the ground, both recognizable as Yoshino's lieutenants. Another one of them —Quan, she thought—was on the staircase between a pair of guards. The fallen lieutenants had been riddled with bullets like they'd run out into the open to draw fire. Cait shook her head. "Stupid. Leave the heroics to the folks with armor."

The guards on the stairs fired at every black-clad figure that came into view. If she'd had her magic, this would have been easy. She grabbed a smoke grenade, then put it back, realizing it wouldn't do any good. They would have thermal or other visual options in those bizarre helmets. She readied herself to charge them.

Explosions came from above, and her head snapped up. She saw the guards and Quan rushing up the stairs. She fired blindly into the room to keep the soldiers' heads down as she dashed after them.

---

The detonations caused all three of them to jump. Yoshino ripped the sword from its sheath, and Kono snapped his gun around toward the sound. Xie pulled the trigger.

Fortunately, her weapon had been pointed at the door and hit nothing important.

Six black-clad figures dropped through the holes that had appeared in the ceiling, and Yoshino commanded, "Attack before they can get set."

That proved to be impossible since the troops fired their suppressed rifles blindly as soon as their torsos were in the room. She and her allies scattered in different directions—Xie to the left, Kono to the right, and Yoshino diagonally across the room toward the door. She leapt onto the table and slid along its surface in a shower of broken dinnerware, bullets striking ahead and behind.

Before the soldiers could get their targeting right, she was in the corner, protected from the others by the body of the nearest. She rammed her sword into his descending body and stabbed it up through his torso to reach his heart. He hit the floor without firing another shot, and she threw her scabbard at the next, who reflexively moved his barrel out of line. It gave her enough time to close, knock the weapon to the side with a crescent kick, and slam him in the helmet with the hilt of her sword.

The one downside of the sword's length was that it was difficult to use in close-quarters combat, and she couldn't create distance without risking getting shot. She stayed near her foe and jabbed the sword hilt into his armor in various places while fending off his barrel. He slammed his helmet forward and caught her in the head, causing her to recoil and take a few steps back. Blood flowed into her eyes from the wound, but she retained enough focus to stab her blade into his throat as he brought his weapon around and aimed at her. He pulled the trigger as he fell, and she took a round in the shoulder that spun her and dropped her to the floor.

Gunfire came from nearby, and the wood around the door's lock splintered. The door slammed open, and two guards, trailed by Quan and Marshal Keane in her hidden identity, flew through. Her lieutenant pointed his gun at the enemy soldiers as he extended a hand to help her up and blocked her from the room with his body. She dropped her sword and shouted in pain as he pulled her up.

The intruders' weapons continued to chatter, and Yoshino watched in horror as a bullet struck Kono in the chest and knocked him down. The marshal shot one of the soldiers in the collarbone several times to take him out of the fight, then drew a dagger from her hip and stabbed it into the back of another's leg. She wrenched it out, and blood spurted.

The man went down with a muffled scream and wrapped his hands around the wound to keep his life from flowing out. A moment later, the last soldier fell. Unfortunately, the two guards who'd rushed in to protect her had as well. Yoshino coughed and said, "Quan, thank you. You can let me go."

Instead, he made an abrupt move and yanked her in front of him, then wrapped an arm around her throat and levered her up onto her toes. He extended his pistol, pulled the trigger, and Xie, in the corner of the room, went down as his bullet struck her in the leg. Kono, from the floor, and Marshal Keane, standing, both snapped their weapons in line with her captor's head. Quan growled, "You move, and she's dead. Put your guns down. One squeeze is all it will take to end her."

Yoshino nodded at Kono. "Do as he says." With her functional arm, which was fortunately on the side away from Quan, she reached up behind her head.

Quan snarled at the marshal, "You too, whoever you are. Figures that Yoshino would have some sort of secret weapon in her pocket. You're her assassin, right? Tell you what. Once your gun is on the floor, your mask can join it."

Keane complied in part and set the gun down. Rather than removing the mask, though, she said, "You've got no way out of here. Let her go, and you get a chance to run."

He laughed. "In less than a minute, I'll have reinforcements. Do what I told you to do and take off the mask, or she dies now."

Keane countered, "You're just going to kill her anyway," and took a step forward. Quan pulled the trigger, but his target spun out of the way and hit the floor before the bullet could catch her. Yoshino used the distraction to snatch an ivory hairpin in her fist, bring it around in a circle, and shove it deep into Quan's neck.

He stumbled to the side, his hand reaching up to the wound, and she ripped the pin out, causing a gout of blood to stain her white robes. Her traitorous lieutenant fell. Kono staggered across the room to her side, showed her the hole in his shirt that revealed the body armor beneath it, and activated his phone to call for reinforcements and a medic.

Yoshino stepped over to Keane. "I owe you thanks once again. I seem to have a lieutenant position open. Would you like to join us?"

The other woman laughed. "Madame Yoshino, I've seen what you do to people who disappoint you. I think not." Yoshino heard the smile in the other woman's words, but then Cait's tone turned serious. "Let me get you out of here."

Kono looked up from where he knelt next to Xie and nodded. "Go."

She complied. As they walked over the bodies on the first floor, she shook her head at the destruction. "If I'd known, I would never have invited them to town."

Keane replied, "It seems to me that they already had you in their sights. You just gave them an excuse."

"Probably true, but still."

"Yeah. I know." When they were far enough away, Yoshino opened a portal, then put her hand on the other woman's arm. "Again, thank you."

Cait nodded. "Any time. Maybe stay out of sight for a while."

Yoshino laughed as she crossed into her safe room. "You can count on it, Marshal."

# CHAPTER TWENTY-FOUR

Victor Huff knotted his tie and turned to head for his private elevator. His partner joined him as he passed through the living room, and he asked, "Did you get any sleep afterward?"

"A little. Being awakened by a guard with news of assassination attempts on notable people in town doesn't do much to contribute to a calm, restful state."

He chuckled. "They won't come after me. My profile is too low."

She snorted. "Don't joke about it. You could be next on the list."

He stopped and gave her a quick hug. "Don't worry. I don't plan to leave the building until things are settled."

A guard stood by the elevator, and the three of them rode down to a floor he didn't often visit. The command center was not on any plans or directories. It was signal- and magic-shielded, although either shield could be switched off at need. He could control every system in the building from this location and had hard-wired communication connections to the internet and satellites available. It was his secret weapon against any enemy he might face.

The people who had done the installation were no longer in Boston, and he'd had them operate under aliases on the paperwork so they couldn't be tracked down by his enemies. They'd also been paid well. Victor had joked at the time about having them killed like those who had constructed the secret room in the pyramids were said to have been, but he wasn't *that* much of a worrier.

The large central table had a display built into it that currently showed scenes from cameras located throughout Boston. At first look, the city seemed quiet. His top people were gathered around it, including his lead infomancer Derek and his elven head of all things magic, Zee. They all looked like they'd been awake since the alert the night before.

He ordered, "Report."

Derek replied, "We've detected no threat aimed at us. It appears someone went after the leaders of the Thorns and Dragons, or maybe they went after each other. What we *can* confirm from sources on the street is that both Carl Winston and Yoshino Kyouka were attacked."

Eliza asked, "Do we have confirmation that either is dead?" Victor chuckled at the combination of hope and bloodthirst in her voice.

Zee replied, "No confirmation. However, neither has been seen in public."

Victor observed, "If someone tried to knock me off, I'd probably maintain a low profile afterward, too." He twisted his head just enough to raise an eyebrow at Eliza, who managed to keep her face still, though he saw the amusement in her eyes. He turned back to the magical, who was also the one coordinating those he'd found and extracted from Perpetuity. "When will our people be here?"

"Tonight. Several are already on the ground. The rest are making their preparations."

Victor considered his options. He'd planned to wait until Friday to put his plan into motion on the assumption that a sudden crisis would hit harder when everyone was looking forward to the weekend. However, Fate had offered him an unexpected dose of chaos, and upon reflection, he couldn't pass it up. "Then it begins tonight. Put all our resources in play."

The others in the room straightened as he gave the command, and his team leaders responded in the affirmative. He and Eliza headed back to the penthouse apartment. When they were alone, she asked, "Are you positive this is the best way to reach your objective?"

Victor laughed. "The best way? No. It will take years to clean up afterward. The fastest way, yes, and that's what matters to me right now. I would say that after the next day or two, my profile should be plenty high enough to get me what I want."

---

Cait had spent Tuesday morning in the office waiting for the news about the attacks the night before to drop. Officially, she had no way of knowing about it, and it would be too risky for her to be the one to mention it first in case someone had noticed the person in the mask.

Around one-thirty, Garrett bolted up from his desk

with a speed that made his chair scrape across the floor and headed for the chief's office. Cait crossed to the coffee maker to eavesdrop and heard him mention the names of both gang leaders. Ten minutes later, Susan stepped out of the office. "Everyone, conference room, now."

They reported as ordered, and the screen at the end of the room came to life. It was filled with outlined boxes filled with heads. The captions read PDA, AET, GTF, and BPD. Sabrina nudged Cait and whispered, "I think the word is out."

Cait didn't reply. The person in the box labeled GTF for Gang Task Force spoke. "Last night, we believe unknown persons attempted to assassinate the leaders of the Thorns and Dragons. We are sure that each gang was attacked, and we have high confidence that Winston and Yoshino were present. Beyond that, we don't know if the attacks succeeded, what prompted them, or who was behind them."

Cait whispered, "We don't know a lot," and Sabrina nodded.

The man on the screen continued, "That would be of concern on its own, but as of right now, the streets are virtually overflowing with gang members."

The representative from the Boston Police Department asked, "More than usual?"

The first man nodded. His expression was deep and dark as if he were both angry and worried. "The task force had no idea this many people were involved in organized crime in Boston."

*That had to hurt to admit.* Cait exchanged glances with Garrett, who shook his head. He apparently hadn't known either. Paul Andrews, in the box marked PDA, asked, "Magical presence?"

The gang task force leader replied, "Unknown, but we know that both the Dragons and the Thorns count magicals among their numbers. At least one of the smaller gangs is exclusively magicals. Several others are suspected of having a mixed membership. Except for the humans-only ones, of course."

Cait blurted, "Wait, it's everyone on the streets? Not just the Dragons and Thorns?"

That no one corrected her for speaking out of turn was a sign of how concerned they all were. The gang task force leader replied, "Every gang color and symbol we know of has been spotted, plus a couple more that we're trying to identify."

The leader of the local AET, Eduardo Val, growled, "What the hell?"

Susan said, "We have no way of telling what's happening right now. However, I think we can all agree that we need to come up with a plan and that none of our people will be heading home until we figure out what's going on in our city."

Cait stepped out of the room as the conversation continued. She dialed Kono but got no answer. She tried her other Dragons contacts, but none were picking up. The meeting broke up, and Sabrina went to her desk and started typing furiously. Cait walked over to peer over her shoulder. "Find something?"

Her friend gestured at the screen. "Useless. The infomancer boards don't have anything either."

"I think this is bad. Do you think this is bad?"

Her friend looked up. "Very. Completely. Definitely. Totally."

Cait crossed the room to the chief's office and knocked on the open door. Susan twisted from where she was typing on her computer. Her expression was calm and focused, which Cait should have expected. "Yes?"

"I'd like to reach out to the Special Operations Group and ask them to be on standby in case we need them. It shouldn't be a big deal, and they won't deploy until we give the word."

Susan didn't even have to think about it. "Approved."

Cait sprinted back to her desk and called Elliott Black. He picked up and said, "Good to hear from you, Spirit."

"Good to be heard from. We've got a ton of hustle and bustle among the gangs in Boston going on right now, including magicals. The chief has approved me asking you to put the teams on standby."

He replied, "Can do. Do you have time to play taxi?"

She thought about what she could accomplish in the office, which amounted to very little. "Let me check with the boss, but I think I can."

---

That night, after darkness fell, Victor and Eliza went back to the command room. He asked, "Are we ready?"

Derek replied, "Yes. We've hacked the city's infrastructure. We'll be able to knock out the power grid and confuse all the other systems at will."

"Excellent." He swiveled his head to look at the leader of his magicals. "And the rest?"

Zee answered, "We have people on the streets dressed as Thorns and Dragons positioned in one another's territory, ready to light it up. Your team is assembled, just waiting for you to give the word."

Destiny settled on Victor's shoulders like a shroud. He knew he was worthy of what he sought. "All right then. Initiate Phase One."

# CHAPTER TWENTY-FIVE

Cait had decided to stay at SOG headquarters with the teams. They had donned their fatigues but not their gear, so when the word came from Sabrina that fighting had broken out in the city, they ran to the locker room to equip. Aza sat beside her as Cait strapped on the pieces of her armor and pulled on her bulletproof vest.

The night promised to be chaotic enough that she opted to wear a helmet despite the distraction it would cause, especially when she used magic. She headed for the armory and retrieved a rifle, a pistol, and several grenades. After a moment's thought, she also grabbed a taser and a reload cartridge and shoved them into a utility pack.

Cait had a feeling that the situation would be deadly serious from the start, but if an opportunity to take someone down nonlethally came, she'd embrace it. Other members of her group chose similar weapons, although Angel also selected a shotgun that was heavy enough that Cait wouldn't be able to wield it effectively without using magic to supplement her strength.

When they were all ready, she opened the portal to the staging point the various units had agreed upon, which was located roughly on the border between Thorns and Dragons territory. A semi-truck was attached to the long trailer that served as a command vehicle for the combined group. Cait ran inside, found the primary and secondary frequencies of the shared force, and relayed them to the team's tech wizard, Julie "Crystal" Schorr.

A moment later, the SOG's earpiece radios tapped into the channel. It was filled with reports of fires and destruction. From the sound of it, both gangs had decided not only to go after the other one's people but everything they owned or protected. She flicked to the channel that was connected to the Paranormal Defense Agency and said, "This is Marshal Cait Keane. What's the situation?"

Natalie Hood replied, "We've got a team of magicals and mundanes in Chinatown, burning down buildings and killing people. Another team is in Thorns territory, doing the same. No word of similar destruction in the rest of the city."

Elliott "Knight" Black grabbed Cait's arm and asked, "Where do we go?"

Cait replied, "Send the other team to Thorns territory. I need to be in Chinatown."

---

In his command post, Victor listened as reports came in over the radio frequencies his infomancers had hacked. His teams impersonating each of the gangs had started the fight, but now the actual members of the Thorns, Dragons, and the city's smaller gangs kept them going, convinced that the city's two largest factions had decided this was the day to have it out. The attempt to kill their leaders less than twenty-four hours before had primed the fuse, and all Victor had needed to do was add a little heat. He muttered, "Time to turn it up to eleven." Louder, he asked, "Is the magical team ready?"

Zee replied, "Yes."

"How long will it take?"

"Ten, fifteen minutes. They've been preparing for hours."

Victor exchanged glances with Eliza, who nodded. She'd been his conscience until things began. She would be his guard and supporter until they were over. "Then get them started."

---

They charged through the portal to find Chinatown in flames. Elliott took immediate command of the situation and deployed his people in their usual teams, arranged them with instructions to defend one another, and ordered an advance. They had to traverse several streets to catch up with the arsonists. The group was a dozen strong, dressed in the red and black colors associated with the Thorns. They marched down the street, the ones on the outside shooting rifles at every person they saw while those in the center tossed fireballs at the buildings.

Elliott paused the group at the end of an alley and ordered, "Devil, Spirit, you've got the left half of the street. Best angle is probably on the other side. Brain, you're with me on the right. Everyone else, covering fire to protect the action."

Cait tapped Angel on the arm, and they scuttled across the street under her veil. Unfortunately, the person in the back of the procession turned while they were halfway across and apparently saw something that spooked him. He shouted a warning and fired his weapon randomly in their direction. Cait snapped up shields in front of her position and around her allies, warning, "Magical shields up." That would stop anyone from using a weapon that didn't have anti-magic ammunition loaded.

She raised her rifle and dropped one of the people on her side. Angel did the same, and then gunfire was everywhere. It smacked into the car they'd hidden behind after passing through the shield she'd placed in front of it. She warned, "The enemy has anti-magic ammunition. Stay behind cover."

Her shields offered them complete protection from the magicals' efforts to hit them with fireballs but required her to spend several moments intercepting the spells aimed at her team and the nearby buildings with frost magic.

As the battle continued, a group of people in the colors of the Dragons, green and gold, emerged from shattered storefronts and mowed down the remaining Thorns with rifle fire. They melted away before Cait's allies' bullets could reach them. She winced, then growled at herself for caring. Yoshino had apparently chosen this fight, which meant any loyalty Cait felt to her was invalid while her team was involved.

From above the buildings, Aza sent, *Another group two*

*streets up and one to the right.* She shared that information with the team, and Elliott got them moving.

She sent back, *Do you see Yoshino or recognize any of her people out here?*

Aza replied, *No. Nothing. Do you think she started it?*

*I sure hope not.* Cait didn't know what to believe. None of this made sense. The Dragons weren't this aggressive. She'd guess it was the Cui Siwang again, but they'd always shown up in black uniforms, and besides, this wasn't their style. For the Thorns to do something this stupid would be out of character.

As the thought passed through her mind, she examined it a second time. Carl had never been the most stable person, and if he suspected the Dragons had attacked the night before instead of the Cui Siwang, it might have pushed him over the edge. They caught up to the next group and discovered they were apparently being smart and using magic detection of some kind. As soon as her team emerged from the alley, magic flew at them, and Cait was forced again to focus only on shielding them from the magic barrage. She sent, *Aza.*

He replied, *Nonlethal?*

Cait winced in regret at what she was about to say. *No. They're attacking innocents. Burn them.*

It was a sight to behold. Aza was full-sized when he swooped down, hidden by his camouflage scales, and strafed the group with fire breath. A couple managed to shield, but most hadn't been prepared for an attack from above. The two who survived spun to engage the dragon, and Angel and Cait stood and triple-tapped them, ending their targets' concerns forever.

Kingston "Royal" Foster said, "Let's let the dragon do the rest of the work. It seems a lot safer that way."

Cait was about to reply, but her comm crackled. Sabrina said, in a weird, confused tone, "Cait?"

She replied, "Here."

"We have a problem."

Surprised laughter escaped her, and she retorted, "Only one?"

"There's a giant dragon in the Thorns' territory."

Cait frowned. "Say that again."

"There is a huge, massive, enormous dragon in the Thorns' territory. Like, building-sized."

Her mind couldn't produce anything intelligent to say. "What's it doing?"

"Destroying everything it sees."

Cait's brain lurched back into motion and shouted, "Everyone form up. We've got a monster on the other side of the city to deal with." As they ran toward her, Cait pushed up her sleeve to expose the bracelet Cara from Diana Sheen's team had given her. She drew an X on the flat part with her finger and held it there for the required three seconds. Then she opened the portal, and they all ran through to the Thorns' territory to face the monster that awaited them there.

# CHAPTER TWENTY-SIX

Cait stepped through the portal. Her landing point put her, Aza, and her SOG teammates three blocks from the dragon, and when she saw it, she wished she'd increased the distance. The massive creature filled a four-lane street and then some and towered at least twenty stories. Buildings near it and behind it were either on fire or had been converted partially or fully to rubble.

Sirens were everywhere, and she hoped the alert had gone out soon enough that most of the innocents in the affected area had gotten out of range before the monster reached them. Lights flickered, then went out around her as Boston's electrical grid failed. Her comm clicked as it switched to a backup frequency, an indication that power to the city's unified communication system had also dropped.

Beside her, Angel muttered, "What the hell?"

Cait laughed darkly. "It's obviously a Chinese dragon. Try to catch up, Devil." His lack of reply to her jab showed how much the impossible sight had affected him. AET units were deployed on both sides of the street and fed a steady stream of bullets into the dragon, but the creature seemed unmoved by the martial display. She imagined the heavy rounds were ricocheting off its scales but couldn't see the monster clearly enough to be sure since its fire breath had created a miasma in front of it that blocked her view.

A portal opened next to her, and Cait skipped to the side in alarm. Diana Sheen walked through, followed by Cara, Hank, and Rath the troll with his bright purple hair. Aza swooped down and landed beside them, then he and Rath went through their greeting ritual, which involved hands slapping paws, shoulder bumps, a chest thump, and lots of other rambunctiousness. It made her smile despite the danger that had brought them together.

The agents were dressed in their usual heavy body armor, and each was equipped with a rifle and pistols. Hank also had a heavy shotgun in his hands. Cara's backup weapons were the daggers at her belt and Diana's the sword sheathed across her back. The agents' leader said, "Well, that's not something you see every day. When you set off the alarm, I thought you'd need help with a fugitive. This is a bit much."

Cait laughed. "What can I say? We do things big here in Boston."

Cara raised a device that looked like a walkie-talkie, and a moment later, Kayleigh, the team's tech, spoke in her comm. "Okay, boss, I hijacked their frequencies. You're in."

Diana snapped, "Who's Keane's boss?"

Elliott's voice replied, "I am."

"I'm not sure Cait told you about us, but we're government, we're well-armed, and we've got magic. Tell us how we can help you."

He said, "No grand strategies. According to the AET, the thing has refused to be led away. It doesn't seem to have any objective other than smashing things and setting them on fire. Just do your best to keep the collateral damage down while we try to kill it. Our backup plan is a squadron of fighters from the nearest Air Force base, but I'd kind of like to avoid that."

Diana nodded. "Same here. That would be bad. Okay. Rambo, bombing run. Get Scales to take you up high. Croft, left side. Hercules, right side. I'm going in after it." She stomped toward the dragon and raised her rifle to shoot at it despite the distance.

Cait announced, "Devil, stay with these guys. I'm heading in with Diana." She rushed to catch up with the other woman.

In her earpiece, Hank said, "Glam, we'll need the combat drone from the mobile armory. Let me know when you're ready, and I'll give you a portal to fly it through."

The tech replied, "On it."

Cait pushed away the concern that threatened her composure. Even with the agents and every force in the city arrayed against it, taking down the massive monster hit the logical portion of her brain as an impossible task.

---

Rath ran away from the others to get some space for the maneuver and leapt onto the dragon's back. He fit perfectly in his three-foot size when the dragon was at his biggest.

They'd learned that through wrestling matches, although climbing up on him was a bad plan during a bout. He'd learned *that* when the dragon flopped over on his back to squish him.

He wrapped his hands around Aza's neck as the dragon flew up. He couldn't hear the dragon when he spoke since Cait wasn't around to interpret, but he maintained a conversation, assuming what his temporary mount would reply. "So, this looks like it will be a hard one. Like, *Godzilla versus King Kong* hard, but without the giant monkey. Could you grow that big? I can't. I can only do about eight feet."

He spotted a good perch and pointed at a nearby building. "Up there. That'll be perfect." The dragon angled toward it. "I'm going to fly down and drop a bunch of grenades on its head. If I'm lucky, I'll get a couple in its mouth, and this whole thing might be over." Aza lurched, and Rath squeezed harder. "You should go for its eyes. If I were you and had those claws, I'd do that."

He tilted his head to the side. "Do you think I could get dragon armor? Like, do you guys have extra scales or something?" Aza landed on the rooftop, and Rath climbed off. He said, "Gwen, chart me a path." The artificial intelligence in his suit drew a serpentine line in his goggles, very much like a video game. It displayed rings that he had to fly through to reach his destination. The AI had been listening in on the way up. She was always listening and knew he was going to aim for the head.

His flight path would take him around it one full time before he could escape. The attack would be dangerous, but Rath had never backed away from danger and wasn't about to let the oversized menace down the street make him start. "Air currents, please." Lines representing them appeared as an overlay on his display. His route took them into account, so he didn't really need to see them, but he could use them more effectively if he knew when they were coming.

Loft was always a problem during Rath's airborne escapades. His flight gear could only glide, and as much as he begged for a rocket or some other form of propulsion, everyone kept telling him it was impractical. He thought they were afraid to trust him with anything like that. *Which is crazy. I'm an excellent flyer.*

He checked his bandoliers to make sure the grenades were ready to be pulled, then raced to the edge of the roof and jumped. He slapped the button on the center of his chest to expand his wings, and they flicked out of the rectangular compartment on his back. A gust of wind bumped him up with a stomach-lurching thump, and he shouted in pleasure at flying again. It was one of his most favorite things. A moment later, Aza was beside him. Rath called, "Good formation."

The dragon flew a barrel roll to show off, and Rath copied him, laughing. A soft chime pinged in his ear to signal that he was nearing the beginning of his attack run, so he focused on the mission. His path brought him to the monster's head without alerting it since the barrage of bullets and other attacks from below kept it occupied.

He pulled out two grenades and popped the pins with his thumbs. It held only the explosive version, which was standard practice when an alarm like the one Aza's partner had triggered went off. He dropped them as he flew above the edge of its skull. The weapons were set to activate on impact, and when they detonated, he was curving around the other side of the thing's head to release two more.

An additional pair followed before he was forced to yank sharply to the right, off his planned path, when the dragon reared up and swung one of its paws at him. It breathed fire as well, but Aza flashed between him and the dragon to block it with his outstretched wings. Rath adjusted his flight to keep the friendly dragon between him and the nasty one and angled toward the ground. Diana asked, "You okay, Rambo?"

He replied, "Perfect, but the stupid giant jerk dragon didn't care about my grenades."

---

Carl Winston paced his bunker as he pulled on the last pieces of his gear, unable to stay motionless. He'd received news of the supposed Dragons' attack on his territory the moment it happened but hadn't believed a word of it. He knew in his bones that Huff had been behind the attacks the night before, and he didn't see Yoshino as capable of having moved this quickly to take advantage of it.

When he'd heard about the massive dragon that had appeared in his territory, he was certain it could only be Huff. If Yoshino had been up to something that big, his spies would've heard about it. His intelligence expert, or former intelligence expert, had been very good at her job. The Dragons could never have surprised him like this, and Yoshino was too honorable to inflict such damage on the city.

That meant it *had* to be Huff. He took a moment to curse because his plans against the man hadn't started sooner, then threw that worry away. He checked his pistols to confirm they were unstrapped, made sure his throwing knives were ready, and slid a pair of machine pistols into holsters on his chest.

Next, he donned his glasses. His suit linked to them and gave him a customized information display. He spoke the command to activate his earpiece and portaled out of the bunker. He'd made a point during his first days in Boston to find locations from which he could observe the city or, as tonight, use his flight suit to reach important areas. As soon as they'd begun planning against Huff, he'd remembered those days and put this option in his back pocket as a way of reaching him. People rarely considered their vulnerability to an attack from the air. He asked, "You've got the drones ready?"

The amused voice of the infomancer he'd worked with throughout his career with the Syndicate replied, "For the tenth time, yes."

"You're sure they can break the windows?"

"Unless transparent metal is a thing, yes."

Carl broke the lock off a security grate covering a ladder with a burst of force magic and started climbing. "They're loaded with anti-magic?"

The other man groaned. "How many times have we worked together? Of course they're loaded with anti-magic."

Carl replied, "Excellent. I'll be in position in less than a minute."

"You give the go, and it's on."

Cait did not enjoy being in her current location, which was directly under the upraised torso of the massive Chinese dragon. Beside her, Diana slashed at it with her sword, which scraped across its scales before it bit in and drew blood from their foe. Admittedly, it was only a little, but it was the first damage they'd accomplished. Bullets had done nothing, even from up close.

Cait and Diana were both using their magic entirely for defense, each afraid the dragon would crash down on them. It was a difficult trade-off. To be near enough that they could engage with magical weapons meant they risked being turned into pancakes. She drew Eclipse and stabbed it into the dragon. It managed to pierce its hide but didn't sink in very deep. She called, "I'm not sure we're making a dent in this thing."

Diana slashed it with her blade again and cursed. "I agree. We're only breaking its protection when we get lucky."

Kayleigh's laughter sounded in their ears. "Well, pathetic people, never fear. The combat drone has arrived to save you."

## CHAPTER TWENTY-SEVEN

Cait followed Diana as she ran for safety. When they reached cover, the agent pulled an object from her belt and handed it to Cait. "Glam, drone to my tablet."

The screen on the device lit up, showing the combat drone's view as it flew toward the huge dragon. It was still several blocks from its quarry. Hank's comment was preceded by a bout of coughing, doubtless from the smoke that now covered the sky. He said, "Bullets haven't done much against this thing."

Glam chuckled. "But your guns are so small. Mine, on the other hand, are not." Ammunition counts on the left and right bottom of Cait's screen spun down as the drone's rotating guns fired. Tracer rounds made it look like the drone was armed with laser beams. The bullets smashed the dragon in the head and chest. It reared up with a bellow and looked for a frightening moment as if it might topple over backward.

Instead, it whipped out a paw far more quickly than she would've expected it could to swipe at the drone. The craft dipped to avoid it and circled away. The dragon roared and bathed it in fire, but the equipment was hardened to withstand it. Out of range of the fire breath, it turned to fly in again. Kayleigh sounded angry. "Okay, you want to be like that, you bastard? Let's do it."

Smoke trailed from the drone as four rockets shot out of it. They curved to close in from different sides, although the street didn't allow them much room for separation. The dragon reared and swatted at the missiles, intercepting one that exploded on impact. Two struck it in the chest, and one impacted its skull. The dragon dropped to all fours and swayed back and forth. Kayleigh crowed, "Take that, scumbag."

The last thing Cait saw on her borrowed display was the dragon's spiked green tail as it whipped up over its back and slammed into the drone. She looked up and saw the explosion and the pieces of metal that rained down on the ground as a result. Diana said, "Well, there's that. Plan B. Have all non-magicals keep up the barrage, if only as a distraction. Magicals, front and center to hit it with your strongest stuff."

Diana walked forward, and Cait matched her step for step. Cara and Hank dashed up to fall in line beside them. Several other uniformed people she didn't recognize from the AET and a couple of police officers in riot gear joined them. When they reached maximum striking distance, Diana said, "Fire is probably a no-go, but anything else you've got, let that thing have it."

Diana opted for shadow, which inspired a small shudder in Cait despite her training and experience. She chose lightning and blasted its chest. Others used frost, which seemed like a logical choice, and one optimist tried force, which accomplished nothing. Cait maintained the lightning barrage with her left hand and prepared defenses with the other.

When the dragon fired breath at them, she hurled a blast of frost magic to counter it. Several others had seen the need to act as well, and the fire didn't reach them. They continued their attack, and the dragon roared in anger.

Diana called, "I'm pretty sure we're hurting it. Keep it up, and if any more magicals are hanging around, get them here."

---

Victor was still in the operations room, listening to the ongoing chatter over the emergency channels. He'd thought that when this moment came, he'd revel in it. Instead, he heard each report of damage to the city he loved as if it were a knife stabbing into his side. His mouth was set in a grim line, and he listened carefully to each word from his subordinates and every sound from the radios to judge the right time to act.

He'd been told that both the dragon and the gang conflicts would become self-sustaining but hadn't really believed it. Reports of continued fighting in Chinatown confirmed it, though. The Thorns must have had people there waiting for such a moment. The Dragons must have had the same in their enemy's territories.

Finally, he couldn't listen to it anymore. He ordered, "Have any of our people who are still active in Dragons and Thorns territory disengage and come back to us." The others looked relieved at his words.

His magical lead asked, "Should I send the magical team we brought in home?"

Victor frowned. The people he'd recruited through Perpetuity were powerful and appeared to be loyal, but he didn't trust them the way he trusted those in this room. He exchanged glances with Eliza, who had a doubtful look on her face. She was apparently also concerned about the potential vulnerability they posed. He shook his head as he met the other man's eyes again. "No. They know too much, and they're not ours like our other people are. See that they wind up casualties of the battle."

The other man nodded. "Yes, sir."

Feeling ill at what he'd set in motion, Victor took Eliza's hand and headed for the elevator. By the time it reached the penthouse apartment, he had reassured himself that what he was doing was, in the end, going to be worth whatever it cost. He walked over to the window and stared out at something he'd never seen before: large portions of Boston in flames. He didn't have a line of sight on the dragon his people had created but could see the blazing buildings near its position. *Soon. It will be over soon.*

---

Cait grew more despondent with each blast of lightning she threw at the dragon. They seemed to have achieved a momentary stalemate, but she worried that it was more because the monster was trying to figure out how best to squash them than for any other reason. *We need more power.*

Aza, who had swooped in to attack the thing's eyes several times, sent, *Too bad we're not in Ireland.*

Cait thought back to her experience on Croagh Patrick, then lowered her inner barriers and reached out with her power. Her attack fell away as she put more energy into the search, and she allowed her defenses to dissipate as well, counting on the others to protect her. It took her several seconds to find a hint of what she'd felt on the mountain, and it was distant.

The line ran from the west to the south from where she was. It was far away, but it was there. She could sense it, which meant she could use it. She sent to Aza, *Protect me,* and threw her consciousness into the earth. It took an unknown amount of time to make direct contact with the line and longer still to create a conduit to it.

When she opened her eyes again, it was unclear how long the battle had been going on, but nothing major had changed. Cait walked to Diana and touched her on the shoulder to extend the magic connection to her. She ran down the line and did the same with each of the others, not knowing another way to share it. When she got back, Diana said, "I don't know what you did, but don't stop doing it. That's amazing."

She laughed since she knew exactly what the other woman was feeling. She felt it too—the same sensation of abundant power and health she'd had on the mountain. Diana called, "Lightning seems to work the best, followed by shadow. So, if you're good with lightning, hit it with that. If you're better with shadow, use that. This time, we don't stop blasting until it's down."

The agent counted down, then Cait hurled a seamlessly

combined blast of lightning and shadow. It met the power of the others in the center of the dragon's chest, and the massive creature stiffened. It wobbled for several moments, then roared at them and blasted fire over them. Their shields were adequate to defend against the assault, and they maintained the attack.

The standoff lasted for ten seconds that felt like an eternity, then the giant dragon fell forward and hit the ground with a crash, its eyes closed as if it were unconscious. After several more seconds, they allowed their attack to falter. The dragon shimmered, then vanished. Cait growled, "What the hell?"

Diana shrugged. "Maybe the power flowed through to knock out whoever conjured it. No way to tell. I'm just glad it's gone."

She nodded. Now that the dragon was no longer filling the air with its rage, the sound of gunfire from a few streets away was audible. "Looks like we have more folks to clean up. Thank you so much for your help with that thing."

Diana laughed. "Oh, don't worry. We're not leaving until the party's over. Let's go see what craziness awaits us over there."

As they ran, Cait checked in with Elliott, who informed her that the entire SOG was fine and was engaged with gang members nearby. She took the lead and ran in that direction, confident that her Special Operations Group and Diana Sheen's team would be more than adequate to meet any remaining threat.

*After all, we brought down that dragon together, right?*

## CHAPTER TWENTY-EIGHT

Carl reached the top of the tower and looked down over the city. Massive flames had broken out in territory that belonged to the Dragons and even bigger ones in his former gang's part of town. He sighed inwardly at the frustration of considering the Thorns as existing in the past.

He'd always been good at leaving things behind, but he was still having a hard time letting go of the loss of Cynthia, and she was bound up with the gang. He'd believed in that partnership and had thought they would accomplish great feats together. He growled at himself, "None of that is important right now." A verbal command reactivated his comm, and he said, "Final check."

The infomancer replied, "Ready to go, boss."

Carl instructed his suit to display the range and direction of his target, jumped into the air, and spread his arms wide. The flight suit was a standard piece of Syndicate equipment, and he'd trained both on mountains and in cities. His power gave him the added ability to gain loft by using force magic to push off things when he got close to them, which he'd also done enough times that it was now routine.

He didn't need to think about the flying, so he turned his attention to what was going to come next. "Status."

His infomancer said, "I have thermal readings on two people near the west windows."

Carl smiled. He'd figured Huff would be watching to revel in the chaos he'd caused and was pleased to be proved correct. "Then shoot out the south ones, and I'll approach from that direction."

The other man's tone was dubious. "Are you sure? I could just end this now."

"No one kills Huff but me. Do what I said."

"Right on. You're the boss, boss."

Carl had a locator beacon going for the infomancer so he could arrange the proper timing. As he descended toward his target at what seemed like an alarming speed, his nervousness grew. The windows ahead looked very solid. He clamped down on the thoughts with an act of will and trusted all would be well.

The barrage of bullets struck the glass just before he arrived and shattered it. He flew in and skidded across the floor. The first thing he saw was a pair of guards standing near the door, and he summoned a blast of force to take them out. That is, he tried to, but his magic failed to come. *Uh-oh.*

Cait crouched behind the cover of a large mailbox and traded fire with a small group of gang members while Diana and Cara moved around to flank them. They'd reached the point where they could consider the use of nonlethal options, and Sheen's team had brought along taser grenades. They threw one, and the sizzle was followed by a lack of gunfire. She called, "Good work."

Her earpiece crackled with a new connection, and Sabrina's voice filled her ear. "Gunfire at Victor Huff's apartment."

"Source?"

"Looks like drones. I can't be sure. My drone is closing now." Cait had asked Sabrina to keep an eye on several things during the fight but knew she'd stretched the info-mancer's resources thin. The other woman cursed. "They just shot down my drone. It's definitely other drones."

Cait sent, *Aza, Huff's apartment. Go take a look.* They'd scoped it out when the man's name had first come up in their investigation. The dragon had the recon advantage since he could fly up and see inside. She ran through her options, finding none that would get her to the penthouse to find out what was going on but knowing it was important that she did. Huff was one of the town's major players.

Something occurred to her. "Glam?"

The tech replied, "Yeah?"

"Can those heavy drones of yours support a person's weight?"

The other woman laughed. "I'm sure of it. They have power to spare."

"I've got a favor to ask."

Carl yanked out his machine pistols and started spraying even before his slide ceased. The bullets caught one of the guards and dropped him. The other raised his pistol, and Carl reached for his shield before remembering that his magic didn't work. He threw himself to his feet and took the rounds aimed at his head in the chest. The three impacts hurt but failed to penetrate his armor.

Being a Syndicate operative was a hazardous job, and the organization ensured its people were protected by the latest technology.

He ran forward and knocked the gun out of the man's hand with a crescent kick, grabbed him by the throat, and kicked his legs out from underneath him. The man hit the floor. Carl knelt and growled, "What do I need to know about the security in this place?"

His foe spat blood in his face. "Bite me."

Carl stood and shot him instead. The hiss of an elevator opening caught his attention, and his head snapped up to see something metal coming out of the wall. He dove to the side as the drone spun and fired at him with a machine gun. He rolled, came up running, and maneuvered to keep one of the room's two massive support pillars between him and it. The machine pistol in his right hand fell to the floor as he released it to grab a grenade. He primed and released it, then kept moving around the column.

His timing was flawless. The drone reached his former position as the grenade exploded. Pieces flew, then fell to the floor. Carl drew his right-hand pistol and surveyed the room. He'd been facing away from Huff when he had fought the guards, and apparently, the man had fled the room. He yelled, "Victor, where did you go? I'd like to have a word with you."

To ensure he didn't get another surprise, he wired the entry doors and the elevator with explosives. Anyone else who thought they would crash his private party was in for a rather rude welcome. He holstered his remaining machine gun, drew his left-hand pistol, and headed for the part of the apartment he hadn't yet visited.

---

Cait muttered, "This is so stupid," over and over as a mantra as she climbed onto the drone that had just come through Cara's portal. She whipped force bands around it and gathered the ends in her hands to hold herself in place.

The agent patted her arm. "You spend too much time with us, and you get like this. You'll be fine."

Cait crouched and forced her voice to be steady. "All right, Glam, let's do it." The drone lifted off the ground, found its balance, and headed into the air.

Aza sent, *People are shooting inside the apartment.*

She replied, *Stay clear until I get there.* The next minute was spent chanting her mantra until the drone delivered her to the broken windows of Victor Huff's apartment. She stepped off her transport, spotted movement on the far side of the room, and shouted, "Stop. You're under arrest."

A male replied, "You have *got* to be kidding me," and Carl Winston stuck his head around the corner.

She drew her pistol and snarled, "What the hell are you

doing here? Wait, it doesn't matter. Lay on your face and put your arms behind your head."

Instead of complying, he raised his gun and shot at her. She flinched aside to evade but needn't have bothered since Aza flashed between them to block the bullets. Cait curved around a damaged pillar in the middle of the room and came out the other side, ready to shoot, but a flash bang went off at that instant. She cursed as she dove back into where she thought cover was. Aza joined her a moment later, a physical presence covering her with his body and wings.

As her hearing started to return, she heard an explosion from deeper in the apartment and rushed toward it to investigate.

# CHAPTER TWENTY-NINE

Carl had taken cover around a corner as the grenade detonated and rushed through the shattered doors a moment afterward. Beyond was a bedroom that would have qualified as a whole apartment in a less affluent domicile. The area he was in was a sitting room with chairs, side tables, and a stereo system that was as much a piece of art as technology. To the left was an open space that held a gigantic bed, and to the right, a doorway that doubtless led to a closet and bathroom, and maybe a sauna or lap pool, given the rest of the chamber.

Huff was in the bedroom, and Carl's eyes locked on him. He stood at the foot of the bed with his hands behind his back, looking calm. Carl took a step in that direction and snarled, "You."

The other man offered a cold smile. "It's been a while, Mr. Winston. I was sorry to hear about your partner. Such a loss."

Carl jerked his pistol up and pointed it at the man's face. "You *should* be sorry. You killed her."

Huff's expression changed slightly, but Carl didn't have an opportunity to figure out why. The former Thorns leader sensed movement at his back and threw himself to the right, figuring it was the marshal sneaking up on him. When he came out of his spin, both pistols were pointing at his opponent. His surprise at seeing the woman in the red dress caused him to delay pulling the triggers.

His hesitation gave her the opportunity to act, and she whipped a combat baton she'd been hiding behind her leg into one of his pistols. The blow knocked it out of his hand and into his other gun, and his finger tightened reflexively, but the impact sent the bullet off target. Carl stepped backward to avoid her backhand slash and drew the combat knife from his lower back. It was serrated on one edge, sharp on the other, and pointed for stabbing.

He held it reversed along his right arm so he could slash or stab with it. The woman sliced the baton at his face, and he leaned back to avoid it. A quick advance and cut from right to left with his weapon caused her to retreat. He took a half-step back in anticipation of another baton strike, but his opponent spun down into a kick that knocked his feet out from under him.

Carl hit the floor, rolled, and narrowly escaped the baton as it slammed down next to his head. He scrambled away, regained his feet, and searched for his pistols, which were too far away to retrieve. She'd advanced with his retreat and slashed the baton at him again, which forced him to evade. He backed away and kicked a table aside so he'd have room to move, but her next swings pushed him into a corner.

Fortunately, he'd planned to go that way. When her

next attack flashed in, he darted to the side and brought his left hand around to pin the wrist that held the baton against the wall. He twisted and slashed low with the knife, but she blocked with her fist and caught his hand with a blow that numbed his fingers and caused him to drop his blade.

The baton followed it to the floor as she wrenched her arm away, and the woman stepped back with a smile. "Surely you can do better than that."

"Count on it." The clock in his head was ticking loud enough to give him a headache. The marshal would doubtless arrive soon to cause trouble, and he had to kill Victor Huff before that happened. Plus, his escape had become questionable. With her in the outer room, he wouldn't be able to leave the way he'd entered.

He'd spotted floor-to-ceiling windows behind Huff in the bedroom and assessed those as his most likely option. It would be a dangerous launch with the flight suit, given the proximity of other buildings, but he was fairly certain he could achieve control before he splattered on the ground. If he couldn't, that would be a better ending to his story than being caught by the marshal.

He surged forward and landed a punch in the woman's stomach that caused her to fold over as she lost her breath. He dashed for the bedroom, determined to find Huff and end him. The man hadn't moved. Carl grabbed his foe's shirt and jacket in one hand and pulled back his right fist for a punch. The first would go to his face for pleasure. The second, into his throat, for keeps.

Huff's eyes widened, and with a curse, Carl spun him around and pushed him in the direction of the charging woman. She threw her arms out wide and danced sideways to avoid her boss. He charged past the duo, grabbed his blade, and spun. She was there, and he slammed the pommel into her solar plexus, then punched her in the face with his free hand.

She reached for him as she fell, her expression filled with shock, and scratched his cheek as he landed the punch. He stabbed the blade forward, but she twisted away. Instead of plunging into her, it slashed her and cut a slice in her dress. Blood flew as she collapsed.

Carl reached up to touch his cheek, saw blood on his fingers, and scowled. "I'll have a memory of tonight, at least for a while. Seems appropriate." He took a step toward Huff, noted his expression, and wondered why the man was smiling. Then his body stopped listening. The effect started high but quickly reached his legs. He collapsed, unable to scream in anger at the wicked turn of fate.

---

Cait rushed into the bedroom and found Victor Huff standing over Carl Winston with a gun pointed at the fallen man's head. On the bed was a woman in a red dress, her face and torso bloody. Cait shouted, "US marshals. Put the gun down."

Victor's head snapped around to look at her. The expression on his face was petulant, as if he were a child and she'd taken a toy away. His gun didn't move, and she said with a slow calm, "Mr. Huff. Winston is down. Any action you take is no longer self-defense, and I'm wearing a body cam that's broadcasting to my team's infomancer. Put your weapon on the floor."

It was a lie, but honesty faltered in the face of the life-and-death situation she faced. She didn't have good cause to shoot Huff, and the anti-magic emitter in his home prevented her from blasting him into unconsciousness as she so desperately wanted to do. He complied, and when he straightened, she grabbed the first aid pack from her belt and tossed it to him. "Go help your girlfriend before she bleeds out." His eyes widened as Aza stalked into the room, and the reaction made her want to see what it would be like if the dragon rushed the man. She sent, *Aza, keep an eye on that scumbag.*

The dragon replied, *Can I burn him?*

*I'm thinking about it.* Cait knelt beside the fallen assassin. She looked into his eyes and saw that he was conscious, but his body was locked into a rictus. She imagined it was quite painful. *Serves you right.* She reached to her belt for the metal case and whispered so quietly that only he would hear it, "I should just let you die, given all the damage you caused with this attack on the Dragons. How the hell did you create that dragon, anyway?"

His head rocked slightly from side to side. She opened the case and pulled out an injector. "If this works, you owe my sister a birthday gift every year for the rest of her life." She shoved its flat end against his neck, probably harder than she needed to, and hit the button to fire the needle and discharge the antidote. Then, figuring she had no reason not to, she gave him two more doses. *Stabbing him is fun. I wish I had another dozen.*

His body sagged as the antidote did its work. Cait

cuffed him and wrapped a zip-tie around his ankles for good measure. When she rose, Victor Huff and the woman in red were staring at her, although his eyes were more focused than hers. He'd gotten her propped up against the headboard, and her head lolled.

Cait said, "Probably a concussion. S, I need a medic up here."

Sabrina replied, "On it."

Victor said, "Thank you, Marshal. I don't know why he attacked us, but I'm glad you came in when you did."

*Sure you are.* Cait shook her head. "I don't know either, but I plan to find out."

# CHAPTER THIRTY

Cait turned her face to the sun and luxuriated in the feel of the wind in her hair. After two weeks, the city was still trying to put the pieces back together, figuratively and literally, and the chaos had been a daily stress. She rode in the passenger seat of Clement's car and ignored the danger of his driving as he wove in and out of traffic.

Aza sat in the tiny back seat. He had leaned over her seat and stuck his head out the window, which she was sure must be interesting for the other people on the road. She could've portaled to her destination instead of riding, but something inside her wanted to make this experience last. Besides, as everyone in the office had pointed out in their last meeting, where prisoners were concerned and Cait was involved, more marshals were probably better.

Clement pulled into the parking lot outside the secure facility. Aza flapped into the sky, and Cait went through the rigorous identification process three times, first at the outer gate, then at the inner door, and then at the guard desk. She'd wisely left all weapons outside, although she was never unarmed when she had her wand bracelets. The facility was a combination of hospital and prison and served as a waypoint for Carl as he awaited transfer to the supermax facility that handled powerful magicals.

A guard left her in the meeting room and closed the door with a loud clang. Her side was bare, with only a simple plastic chair that was bolted to the floor and an alarm button on the wall. She ignored both. The room was bisected by a thick plastic wall drilled with small holes to allow sound to pass through it. The door on the far side opened, and Carl shuffled into the room with two guards in attendance. He was dressed in a hideous orange jumpsuit, his feet were shackled together, and his hands were cuffed in front of him. A bright red backpack finished the look, and she felt the anti-magic emissions it generated.

She smiled at the former and current inmate. "That's one way of making sure you can't use your magic. It kind of clashes with the outfit, though."

He sat in the chair on his side and gave her a surprisingly earnest smile. "It is rather effective and not nearly as complicated as what other places have done to try to deal with magicals."

"Sometimes simple is better."

Carl laughed. "A lesson I will take to heart after my time in Boston, Deputy Marshal Keane. Thank you, by the way, for preventing that bastard Victor Huff from shooting me. I owe you one for that."

He looked calm, even serene. She hadn't seen anything like it since their first meeting, and that had been more condescension than anything. She shook her head at the memory and at all that had happened since. "You can thank me by never crossing my path again."

A wide grin split his face. "After I break out, which I will, I'll think about it."

Cait gave him her professional smile. "This is just a pit stop. You're headed to max security."

His shoulders lifted in a shrug. "So I've heard. The guards seem to like mentioning it. Should prove to be an interesting challenge." He leaned back, seeming pleased with the notion.

She took the seat across the plastic from him. "So, tell me. Why did you do it?"

Despite most of the city's investigative forces trying to figure out what had happened on what was being called "The Night of The Dragon," they'd come no closer to understanding the truth. No one involved was talking. Carl frowned. "Attack Huff? I would've thought that was obvious."

Cait shook her head. "No. Why did you have your people attack the Dragons and the city?"

"That wasn't me."

"Come off it."

He shook his head slowly. "Truly, Marshal. Not me. I was as surprised as anyone. I figured it was Yoshino at first, but when the dragon appeared, that didn't seem like her style."

Cait was quiet, considering his words. *Could he be telling the truth?*

Aza, who was flying around outside the building, laughed in her mind at the thought. *It would be the first time.*

She clamped down on the smile the comment inspired. *True that, buddy.* "Okay then, why did you attack Huff?"

The relaxed look left Carl's face. He crossed his arms and growled, "He shook down the Thorns and had Cynthia killed when we didn't play nice enough. Then he tried to do me and Yoshino the night before the attack."

His pain was evident. It filled every word he spoke, and his eyes were pits of darkness. However, his words didn't make any sense. The truth hit her as she saw the way the false assumptions built on each other. "Wait. You're missing something important. Huff didn't kill Cynthia."

Carl straightened, and his face twisted in anger. "What? Yes, he did."

Cait shook her head. "He wasn't behind it. If anyone was to blame, it was Yoshino, but in the end, it really wasn't her, either." The expressions that cycled on his face were painful to watch. She'd assumed Syndicate assassins would be less connected to their emotions than the norm, but apparently, she'd done so in error.

"Yoshino brought in outside help. They failed in their attack on Cynthia, which Yoshino had ordered, and their organization decided they had to recoup their honor or something. They made the second attempt on Cynthia on their own and were behind the attacks on you and Yoshino."

Carl resolutely replied, "Huff was involved."

She felt sympathy for the man, which was so far beyond what she'd expected from this meeting that she didn't know how to process it. "He really wasn't."

Carl's lip twitched in a hint of a snarl. "I know people, Marshal. That guy is dirty."

"Oh, no argument. You probably don't know the half of it. But Cynthia wasn't him."

Denial warred with acceptance on Carl's face. After a full minute, he grated, "Who was it?"

"The Cui Siwang."

His eyes went wide, then narrowed as he processed the information. "Those bastards." A harsh grin spread across his face. "Thanks, Marshal. Now I have a project."

Cait found his confidence about escaping disquieting. *If he does, I'll never hear the end of it.* "I have to ask. Was the whole Thorns thing worth it?"

Carl leaned back in his chair with a sigh. "No. Rosetta was a right bastard, and he deserved what he got. But the rest, especially Cynthia, no."

She stood. "If you do manage to break out, stay out of my city."

Carl rose and leaned toward the glass. "Or what, Marshal?"

She shook her head but couldn't resist a smile. "It's Deputy Marshal. We're not in the Old West." They shared a chuckle at the running joke, then she dropped her voice. "Seriously. If I see you again outside of prison, you probably won't survive the experience." She turned and headed for the door.

He called, "Sounds like the Old West to me."

She stopped, looked over her shoulder, and smiled. "Maybe it is." She mimed tipping a cowboy hat and left the room.

## CHAPTER THIRTY-ONE

That night, after indulging in some Chinese food even though it wasn't Monday, Cait, Sabrina, Aza, and Princess lounged on the infomancer's couches and watched television while consuming a couple of bottles of wine. Sabrina had insisted on watching TV and had turned to a news channel that was carrying a press conference. The governor of the state stepped to the podium in front of a large crowd of reporters, and Cait asked, "Why are we watching this again?"

Sabrina shook her head as if Cait were the least intelligent person she'd ever met. "Do you not pay attention to the news?"

She stretched out and poked Aza with her feet. "I don't see the point, to be honest. Any news I need I get from our briefings or from you."

The infomancer laughed. "Be quiet and pay attention. You'll care about this."

She grumbled but forced herself upright to focus on the press conference. The governor, a gray-haired man in an expensive dark suit and bright red tie, said, "Victor Huff is a long-standing citizen of Boston. He was relatively unknown to the public before the last two weeks, but the city's political and business leaders have known him for a long time."

Cait leaned toward the TV. "What the hell?"

Sabrina replied, "Shh. Listen."

The governor continued, "But the entire populace knows him now. His interventions to help people hurt during the Night of the Dragon caused by the lawless criminals of our city and to begin the rebuilding process and clearing of the destroyed buildings have been nothing less than tireless. As such, I am proud to appoint him Secretary of the Commonwealth."

Cait blinked. "How did the scumbag manage this? What is a Secretary of the Commonwealth, anyway?"

Sabrina laughed. "He's two heartbeats away from being governor now, and after that, he's in a good position to make a run for President."

A frown replaced Cait's confusion. "All this chaos and destruction was just a grand political ploy. If Carl's right and Huff was behind the Night of the Dragon, it explains a lot. I guess this is what Perpetuity was all about in the end."

Sabrina leaned back with a smile and crossed one leg over the other. "I've done some more digging. It was about a bit more than that. Turns out the organization was doing oodles of extortion and baskets full of influence peddling. A lot of Huff's money comes from that, I bet."

"Well, damn. One more corrupt politician, I guess." Cait's mood dropped, and her next sip of wine was in mourning, not celebration.

Her friend, though, was amused. “Actually, it turns out that Perpetuity is a positive for us rather than for him.” She nodded at the TV, and they watched for several minutes while Victor gave his acceptance speech, during which he played the concerned representative of the people to the hilt. It was nauseating. Cait was about to ask again that they watch something else when the image squeezed down into a box and a news anchor appeared.

Sabrina turned up the volume. The woman on the screen said, “We’ve got breaking news for you tonight. The newly appointed Secretary of the Commonwealth, Victor Huff, has been implicated in a series of illegal activities. Evidence has just been sent to all the major news organizations by an anonymous infomancer collective, and we’re looking into it as rapidly as we can. Here’s what we know right now.”

Sabrina turned off the TV, and Cait barked a laugh. “You just did it again. Damn your need for dramatic timing.”

Sabrina laughed and raised her glass. “I am who I am.”

Cait reached over to rub Aza’s head. The tension she’d felt a few moments before was gone, replaced by a feeling that everything was right in her world. “And you’re the best.”

The infomancer grinned. “I know.”

# EPILOGUE

Aisling sauntered down the main street of Westport in search of a way to be useful. The entire town seemed to be under construction, and while generalized wariness showed on faces here and there, everyone seemed to mostly have recovered from the wolves' attack. She frowned inwardly at the thought. *The survivors, anyway. Not everyone was so lucky.*

After making a full circuit of the town and not finding anything that could use her particular blend of talents, she headed back toward her starting point. She noted movement that seemed out of place, continued walking, and used her magic to drop in on her mechanical bird Grayson, who was perched on a nearby rooftop, basking in the sun to charge its batteries for the flight home.

Through its eyes, she verified that she was being followed by two men, neither of whom was close enough to be a threat. *Let's see what you're up to.* She headed into her favorite coffee shop, ordered a green tea latte, and took a seat in the back that gave her a sight line on the door to enjoy it. If she sensed danger, she'd portal away.

A few moments later, a woman walked through the door and made a beeline for her. She was neither young nor old, probably in her mid-forties, with laugh lines at the corners of her eyes and mouth. Brown hair fell in soft waves past her shoulders. She was dressed in a business suit that fit her trim figure flawlessly, low heels, and a button-up shirt with the top two buttons unfastened. She asked, "You're Aisling Keane, correct?"

"I am. Who's asking?"

"Annika Lind. May I sit?"

Aisling shrugged. "Suit yourself."

The woman took the seat across from her.

"Nice to meet you, Ms. Lind. Now, who *are* you?"

The other woman laughed. She seemed amused but also aloof, which made Aisling think she held an important position. "Hopefully, your new employer."

Aisling blinked. Whatever she had been expecting, that wasn't it. "What?"

"We have a program that identifies up-and-coming talent in the universities. Your name was brought to our attention a while ago, and we've been watching you."

Aisling took a sip of her latte and decided she'd throw it at the woman and make her escape if things got any weirder. "You're creeping me right the hell out, lady."

Lind chuckled. "I'm not concerned. You don't scare easily. That's one of the things we like about you."

Despite how annoying the exchange was, the strangeness of the moment interested her. "Who's we, exactly?"

The woman tapped her perfectly manicured fingernail

on the table. "That will be a much longer conversation that requires some commitments from you, including a nondisclosure agreement. I guarantee you it's more interesting than anything else you've got going."

*Maybe a technomancy think tank? Or a government research project?* "Cutting edge?"

"Oh, I'd say that describes us."

Aisling ventured, "You're with the government, aren't you?"

Lind's red lips stretched in a smile. "Several of them."

Aisling sighed. "Okay, I admit it. I'm intrigued."

Her new acquaintance smiled. "Then let's talk about your future."

## SECRET AGENT WITCH

T.R. Cameron's next series is Secret Agent Witch, featuring Aisling Keane. Book one is *The Spy Who Tamed A Dragon* and it's available at Amazon.

Claim your copy today!

**Aisling Keane is an Investigator with the secretive spy organization known as Dragonfly. Thrust unexpectedly into the field, she and her mechanical Dragon partner are surrounded by danger and intrigue.**

Aisling thought she'd been hired to be a secret agent –

then found that Dragonfly required new recruits, even skilled witches like her, to prove themselves.

One clue leads to the next, and she's assigned to work with Lance Stone on a mission.

Small crimes herald larger ones, and the larger ones suggest a mysterious organization lurking in the shadows.

**When an ally turns into an enemy, Dragonfly has to send a new agent into the field. The mission is simple: Infiltrate, discover and escape.**

But in the secretive world of international crime, nothing is ever really simple. And simple never meant easy.

Fortunately, Aisling's newest creation of technology and magic - a mechanical Dragon about the size of an eagle - has just been improved by her infomancer coworker and given a cutting-edge artificial intelligence. Cait's little sister will need all the help Shimmer can provide.

Despite the workload, she'll still need to find time for family and her coven. A danger is on the horizon, and the coven's guardian is worried. Will it get in the way of Aisling's new job?

**The investigator-turned-agent wouldn't have it any other way.**

For action, magic, snarky banter, martial arts, mystical creatures, and high intrigue, join Aisling Keane on her new adventure!

Claim your copy today!

# AUTHOR NOTES - TR CAMERON

## MARCH 15, 2023

So there we go. Cait's tale, neatly wrapped up. I had planned from the start of the series to end it with something mammoth that brought in both the SOG and the FAM/RAM, and I'm reasonably pleased with how it turned out. If I could go back in time and redo things, I would have brought in Hank's mobile armory in a previous book and then had the eighteen-wheeler in the thick of the final fight.

That I didn't include that can be chalked up to my status as a plotter/pantser. I can only preplan so much before things take on a life of their own. Sometimes that's book to book, other times things literally change direction in the middle of a book and all my downstream planning has to change.

It's pretty consistent with my personality that I plan things enough to get going and then roll with it. My background in live television directing (local stations, nothing fancy) probably has something to do with that. This is where I have to give props to the editing team that keeps me honest!

The *Superstars* conference was amazing. I got to meet some really cool people and learn some immediately useful things. Different vibe than the 20Books conference, which makes it a nice counterpoint. Now I have two chances a year to refill my author tank and learn from those with knowledge to share. I count myself as very lucky.

There will be a short story connected to the Aisling series. If you're already receiving my newsletter, you'll get it there as soon as it's ready. If you're not, you might want to go to the end of these notes and grab the short story associated with this series, which will put you on my mailing list!

I see that series as kind of a combination of James Bond and Mission Impossible, but with the addition of the elements that are part of all my stories. I think you'll really like Aisling's sidekick. I'm already having a ton of fun working up that character.

I'm so looking forward to summer. I'll only be teaching one class instead of two and won't have a new course to prepare for the first time in forever. The kid and I are already booked to see Louis Tomlinson (of One Direction fame), Duran Duran, and Depeche Mode. They're uncertain whether they'll accompany me to see the Cure, assuming I'm lucky enough to get tickets. And I'm anticipating the announcement of a Peter Gabriel concert in my home town. Plus, amusement parks and hopefully a trip to Canada once I get my act together and secure passports.

Cannot come soon enough. Only six weeks to go!

I'm listening to the *Naamah* series by Jacqueline Carey

at the moment. It's lush and vivid, and although I don't love it as much as her other two trilogies in that universe, it's still entertaining and provides me with a different take on writing. I had planned to spend my last 2 audible credits on two specific books and I've managed to completely forget what they were. Gone, like the idea never existed. I wish I could say that's a rare occurrence.

I finished my rewatch of *Battlestar Galactica*. It was so good. The story hung together better for me because of the compressed timeframe, and skipping the storylines that didn't engage me made the whole thing flow perfectly. Still working my way through *Poker Face, The Last of Us,* and *Andor*. The last one is hard. I'm a fan of the Star Wars universe, but *Andor* is just a grind so far. I'll still finish it eventually. I'm kind of in that same place with *Ms. Marvel*. It's lovely, I like the story and love the actors, but it doesn't grip me the way some other Marvel shows have.

Still waiting on my kid to say yes to watching *Wakanda Forever*. Anticipating streaming the latest *Puss in Boots* and seeing *John Wick 4* in the theatre. I also get to see the Louis Tomlinson documentary in the theatre in a week or so.

I finished my replays of *Dishonored* and *Dishonored* 2. It was a genuine pleasure going through and choosing the violent version instead of the stealth version after the stress of the latter. Restarted The Last of Us, but I'm not sure it'll keep my attention. I'd forgotten how dark and difficult it is. I also grabbed *Baldur's Gate 1, Baldur's Gate 2,* and *Planescape: Torment* as a Steam bundle. I loved those games back when they were new. With *Baldur's Gate 3* allegedly on the way this fall, I felt the urge. My party keeps getting massacred by spiders. D&D level 1 characters are not mighty.

Assuming the day job doesn't claim my sanity in the near future, I'll have more nonsense to share at the end of Aisling book 1. And in the newsletter, for those who are subscribed. (If you're reading this, subscribe, seriously!)

Until next month, joys upon joys to you.

**Standard monthly reminders** - If you're not part of the Oriceran Fans Facebook group, **join**! There's a pizza giveaway every month, and Martha and (usually) I and all sort of fun author folks show up via Zoom to chat with our readers. It's a great time, and the community feel to it is truly fantastic. The group is very welcoming and enthusiastic. Oriceran Fans. Facebook. Your phone is probably within reach. Do it!

Important note (that you may have already seen in Books 1 and 2 and 3 and 4 and 5 and 6 and so on): I've written a Cait short story for you to enjoy, about her earliest days with the Special Operations Group. You can find it here: https://BookHip.com/DPKPMTF. It's yours for the minor commitment of signing up for my newsletter. I have absolutely no problem if you want to then unsubscribe for my newsletter. But with social media as quirky as it's been of late, I'd love to have a channel to communicate with you that I can depend upon.

Before I go, once again, if this series is your first taste of my Urban Fantasy, look for "Magic Ops." I promise you'll enjoy it, and you'll get more of Diana, Rath, and company. You might also enjoy my science fiction work. All my writing is filled with action, snark, and villains who think they're heroes. Drop by www.trcameron.com and take a look!

PS: If you'd like to chat with me, here's the place. I check in daily or more: https://www.facebook.com/AuthorTRCameron. Often I put up interesting and/or silly content there, as well. For more info on my books, and to join my reader's group, please visit www.trcameron.com.

# AUTHOR NOTES - MARTHA CARR

## APRIL 13, 2023

I've started a project answering questions for my son about my life. I realized after last year's fifth round of cancer, and then chemo this time that he was expecting me to die sooner rather than later. It's been a lot for him to deal with and there isn't much I can do to make it better, except tell him stories that I can leave behind – eventually. Hopefully, a long time from now. I'm going to let you guys listen in as well.

My author notes for this year are going to be answers to questions and all of you can get to know me better, too. Maybe inspire, maybe give you a laugh along the way.

Today's question is: How did I start over (again and again)? Was it worth it?

Starting over is my specialty for both good and not so good reasons. It's good because it showed me, I was resilient and basically things work out in the end (more on that in a second). It's bad because sometimes I was using starting over as a way to avoid working through something. That last one is okay, too. We learn from everything, nothing is wasted.

Figuring out a new me was a necessity. I grew up without some basic life skills and had been learning through observation. I don't recommend it. It's a very narrow, random way to see the world and lacks something vital - deep connections with others. But it wasn't a trait I learned as a kid and for a very long time I didn't even know I lacked the skills. I blamed myself all the time for not knowing what I was doing, for the doubt, for the fear I wasn't enough, and for not having a more solid path or plan. You can see a lot had to change. A reinvention and starting over from scratch.

First, though, I had to learn to see the world from new angles, which meant a lot of therapy where I spent a lot of my time confused because I was so convinced in what I thought was a belief system, I couldn't hear what the therapist was saying. When an idea is introduced early enough by critical caregivers (parents, teachers, siblings), we take it in as an edict or a belief. In reality, it was someone else's thought introduced as fact and in my case was crowding my ability to think for myself and see the world with new eyes. Those beliefs had to go.

Turns out, I would need some new beliefs that this time I actually chose, to replace the old ones. To even let go at all, I would need so much courage and a belief in something bigger than myself that has my back. I just call it the Universe, but you do you, whatever that means to you.

I was forty-seven when I first really set about changing my belief system and I was terrified pretty much all day and all night long. But I had guides who had walked this kind of path ahead of me and kept encouraging me so I kept trying. Plus, I was tired so backing up and going back to old habits (not beliefs) was no longer acceptable. Thank goodness.

But it was also messy. I said the wrong thing a lot, did the wrong thing, sometimes triumphed with a small change and felt so powerful, and saw things differently because I did things differently.

Turns out these are the three key ingredients. A community that supports you rather than tells you why that won't work out, (my God, that's a pet peeve of mine - predicting failure before something's started. Gah! Don't get me started. The bane of every artist and entrepreneur. We'd still be trying to figure out how to make a wheel work if there weren't people who ignored all the naysayers and did something new and innovative anyway. Okay, it got me started.). A therapist is a really good add-on because they listen with an open mind and don't add in their own stories. You can hear yourself, maybe for the first time.

Second, it takes courage to finally do something different and abandon old habits, old ideas that seemed like truths. It's too easy when things ease up just a little to put off change and keep doing the same thing, but inevitably the road circles back around again and we're left wondering how something 'keeps happening'. We didn't take a different road. Take the different roads, son, even if you have no idea where they're headed. Ask for help from good sources and accept it, take it in and use the help. Be vulnerable. Ignore the movies. Nobody gets anywhere by acting like they did it all, they had no help. They're secretly very lonely people worried about failure.

Last thing, trust yourself and show people the exit who don't trust you and put you down. Run from them. They're life-force suckers who will drain you dry. If you've been doing something that almost gives you what you want, only to fall short again in a pattern, break that pattern and find someone you trust to help you build a new plan. Be bold, be vulnerable, be in community, and choose your path with an openness and willingness to change course as needed. No need to do any of it alone. That changed everything for me. I still had to reinvent myself occasionally, but it was no longer from the ashes, and instead it was to rise to something new with a new challenge. I wish the same for you, but you have to be willing to take those first steps and then keep on going. Love you. Love, Mom. More adventures to follow.

# OTHER SERIES FROM T.R. CAMERON

**Urban Fantasy**
(with Martha Carr and Michael Anderle)

Federal Agents of Magic (8 book series)
Scions of Magic (8 book series)
Magic City Chronicles (8 book series)
Rogue Agents of Magic (8 book series)
Witch Warrior (12 book series)
Secret Agent Witch (8 book series)

**Science Fiction**
(with Martha Carr and Michael Anderle)

Azophi Academy (4 book series)

# OTHER SERIES IN THE ORICERAN UNIVERSE:

THE LEIRA CHRONICLES
CASE FILES OF AN URBAN WITCH
THE EVERMORES CHRONICLES
SOUL STONE MAGE
THE KACY CHRONICLES
MIDWEST MAGIC CHRONICLES
THE FAIRHAVEN CHRONICLES
I FEAR NO EVIL
THE DANIEL CODEX SERIES
SCHOOL OF NECESSARY MAGIC
SCHOOL OF NECESSARY MAGIC: RAINE CAMPBELL
ALISON BROWNSTONE
FEDERAL AGENTS OF MAGIC
SCIONS OF MAGIC
THE UNBELIEVABLE MR. BROWNSTONE
DWARF BOUNTY HUNTER
ACADEMY OF NECESSARY MAGIC
MAGIC CITY CHRONICLES
ROGUE AGENTS OF MAGIC

OTHER SERIES IN THE ORICERAN UNIVERSE:

OTHER BOOKS BY JUDITH BERENS

OTHER BOOKS BY MARTHA CARR

**JOIN THE ORICERAN UNIVERSE FAN GROUP ON FACEBOOK!**

# CONNECT WITH THE AUTHORS

**TR Cameron Social**

Website: www.trcameron.com

Facebook: https://www.facebook.com/AuthorTRCameron

**Martha Carr Social**

Website: http://www.marthacarr.com

Facebook: https://www.facebook.com/groups/MarthaCarrFans/

**Michael Anderle Social**

Website: http://lmbpn.com

Email List: https://michael.beehiiv.com/

https://www.facebook.com/LMBPNPublishing

https://twitter.com/MichaelAnderle

https://www.instagram.com/lmbpn_publishing/

https://www.bookbub.com/authors/michael-anderle

# BOOKS BY MICHAEL ANDERLE

**Sign up for the LMBPN** email list to be notified of new releases and special deals!

**https://lmbpn.com/email/**

For a complete list of books by Michael Anderle, please visit:

**www.lmbpn.com/ma-books/**

Made in the USA
Columbia, SC
14 December 2024

49248982R00150